Upon a MIDNIGHT *Dream*

by

Rachel Van Dyken

Upon a Midnight Dream
London Fairy Tales, Book 1
by Rachel Van Dyken
Blue Tulip Publishing

Second Edition

UPON A MIDNIGHT DREAM
Copyright © 2014 RACHEL VAN DYKEN
ISBN 13 978-1502353511
ISBN 1502353512
Cover art designed by P.S. Cover Design

To my prince, my love, and my daily inspiration… my husband.

PROLOGUE

*That, if then I had waked after a long sleep, will make me sleep again;
and then, in dreaming, the clouds me thought would open and show
riches ready to drop upon me; that, when I waked I cried to dream
again.*
~ William Shakespeare ~

London, England

HE MADE THE GRAVE mistake of looking into her chocolate
brown eyes and cursed himself all over again for having such
fanciful feelings. She wasn't his to fawn over, but someone
else's entirely. Despite the obvious, he was in love or at least it
had felt that way ever since he first set eyes on the girl the year
before. But what good was his love when her heart fully
belonged to someone else?

She was betrothed to his brother, and Stefan hated
himself for it, because it meant that for the rest of his eternity
he had to watch them laugh and smile together. And all the
while, a part of him would die each time her eyes gazed at his
little brother instead of him.

There were three of them. Three brothers in all, and their father, *The King*, as they always referred to him, spoiled them greatly.

His youngest brother had set eyes on Elaina at a dinner party and fallen madly in love. Just as the rest of the family had. With long golden hair and deep brown eyes, she was every man's dream. And the youngest son — the one without the title, the one who was to be a vicar — had won the ultimate prize. The one thing that money and a title could not buy — love.

Stefan looked away. How much pain could a heart take before it was ripped in two? Could unrequited love kill a person's soul with one breath?

His body tensed when she breathed; his breath hitched when she spoke, and his passion ignited when she laughed.

Curse her, and curse his brother Fitz.

It was in moments like this he wished he were more like the second son, James Gregory, without a care in the world. But no, Stefan was too blasted serious for that. He was the heir — the Marquess, living in his own version of Purgatory.

"I will be touring India," Stefan suddenly announced knowing it was poor timing but needing it to be said, nonetheless. His father had made arrangements after seeing Stefan mope around for the last year. It was easily decided upon that a tour of India was just the thing — though at times, Stefan wondered if his father hoped to be rid of him if only to push away the heartache at seeing his eldest son so depressed.

The room went dead silent; his father turned a knowing eye to him. Always perceptive, his brother Fitz gave a brief nod. "Is that what you think is best considering your position, Stefan?"

"I do." Short, clipped tones fell out of his mouth.

Elaina tilted her head and smiled. "What are you about Stefan? You aren't the type to go around seeking adventure.

Wouldn't you be much happier here? Where it is safe? And you can live a quiet happy life?"

If he hadn't already made up his mind, her insulting assessment of his character would have done it for him. "I've made arrangements."

His brother Fitz squinted through his looking glass. "Stefan, this isn't like you. By Jove," he laughed, "you're afraid of your own shadow!"

The room erupted into laughter. All save, his brother James, who with a gleam in his eye said, "I hope you find what you're looking for, brother. And do try to make it back in one piece. You wouldn't want the title passed down to someone such as I."

Stefan Hudson, Marquess of Whitmore and future Duke of Montmouth left that following week and never looked back.

Rosalind Hartwell felt like she was up for auction to the highest bidder. One minute she was engaged to the most ridiculous dandy she had ever laid eyes on and the next thing she knew, a man with darkened skin and sandy blonde hair announced he was the rightful Marquess of Whitmore. Her head was spinning as she grabbed for champagne and winced when she saw the display of male beauty standing before her.

Whoever this stranger was, he made every other male specimen in the room appear gaunt and sick. His skin was dark, his teeth fairly glowing against the set of his square jaw. How had her life come to this?

She looked from side to side; surely someone would step forward and help her? The *ton*, it seemed, had lost their tongues at a very inappropriate time for Rosalind. The only help came from the infamous Lord Rawlings who only moments before had nearly punched the younger brother —

James, her former fiancé — square in the face.

Abby, her dearest friend and now Lady Rawlings, looked in her direction. Rosalind shook her head. No, she would stay put. Let the man get his bearings before he realizes he's betrothed. Saints alive! He just came back from the dead. The last thing any shipwrecked man would appreciate had to be the thought of being chained to a woman not of his choosing. Heavens! He probably hadn't a clue as to his bleak future!

Rosalind adjusted her gloves and waited. The man laughed; the music started. And she continued to wait. That is until the Dowager Duchess of Barlowe looked in her direction, even though Rosalind could have sworn the plant had hidden her.

The bronze man walked towards her. She gulped, and for the life of her, was not able to put anything close to a smile on her face, so stunned was she.

"Lady Rosalind?" He reached for her hand and planted a kiss on her knuckles. Shivers ran down her spine. Fear. That was it. She was afraid. Surely she wasn't attracted to this barbarian!

His next words — though there was no way for her to know it — sealed her fate, her eternity, with that man. "I release you."

Stunned, she closed her eyes to gather herself. "Pardon? Am I some sort of wild creature that begs to be released?"

Something flashed in his eyes before he regained his composure and answered, "Surely, you don't wish to be betrothed to a man you hardly know?"

Rosalind scoffed. "And surely you haven't been away so long as to forget the way that betrothals work. I would shame my family if I broke off our engagement. But your words tell me you are doing this for me, is that right?"

"Yes," he said.

Rosalind clenched her fist, for her arms suddenly felt

heavy, as did her eyes and her legs. Oh no. It was happening again. It could not be happening in the middle of the ballroom! Her tongue became heavy inside her mouth, and swaying on her feet, she managed only to ground out, "As you wi—" before she fell into his arms.

Stefan was at a total loss. A complete and utter state of awe. For never had a women ever fallen asleep while he was talking.

Ever.

And that included the ninety-seven year old Indian woman who smoked that devil's herb all hours of the night.

She managed to stay awake.

His fiancée, however, could not.

"Lady Rosalind?" he asked quietly, though he wasn't sure why. Not only had he caused the greatest scandal known to the ton by showing up alive and breathing at the Season's end, but then his fiancée had promptly fainted in his arms.

"Good heavens! Is she dead?" The Dowager Barlowe fanned herself vigorously as she motioned for help. Several people began whispering behind their fans as they watched the scandal worsen. Lady Rosalind moaned in his arms. The girl looked slightly foxed, though he knew she was nothing of the sort. Merely sleeping.

Just what he needed. More attention. *By all means, gather 'round! Seems I've single-handedly killed the woman I'm supposed to marry. Please, feast your eyes.*

"Have you a place I can bring her?" Without waiting for the affirmative he scooped the tall girl into his arms and strode through the crush to the nearest room he could find. Not wanting to ruin her reputation, but unable to think of any other option, he pushed into the first room the dowager pointed to and promptly dropped the girl onto the leather settee.

"Well, we cannot just leave her in here alone. It isn't to be done!" The dowager continued her incessant fanning, just as the object of their discussion let out a very unladylike snore.

"Is she..." He looked down at the beautiful face. Impossible. He didn't trust his own ears. And then her bow shaped mouth opened, just slightly, and let out a puff of air. "Snoring?" he finished, completely astonished.

Stefan felt around him for a chair, because he dare not take his eyes off the sleeping beauty before him. He finally managed to grab at something and sat.

Directly onto his grandmother.

"Do you mind?" the dowager hissed.

"Apologies," he said, leaping away from his grandmother's' lap. He raked his hands through his long unfashionable hair.

Make that three impossibilities in one night — the last and final blow to his pride being that he was so focused on Lady Rosalind, and consequently unable to think straight, that he landed in his grandmother's lap. Something that hadn't happened to him since he was a lad of eight.

"Well, I'm off then, have a brilliant time, Stefan. It is so good to see you back. I'll be expecting you in the morning, and sorry about all that hoopla out there. After all, I had to play my part. Couldn't let on that I knew you were back before everyone else. Think of what your father would say!"

"You did admirably."

The dowager smiled. "Yes, well, I once tried for the theatre, many years ago, but did you know they don't take to women with opinions?"

"I'm sure they don't."

"It is of no consequence. I shall leave you with—" She pointed, but words ceased. Instead, she shook her head and *tsked* out loud before closing the door behind her.

Stefan's eyes were glued to the door his grandmother had exited, waiting for the inevitable.

The door jerked open once more. "Oh my heavens! I nearly forgot myself. You cannot be alone with her!"

Wonder of all wonders, he's gone for six years and his grandmother, bless her soul, is ever so much the same as before. Why, even birds flying about drove her to distraction.

And he loved her to a fault. "Well, Grandmother, I can promise you that I'll be the perfect gentleman. Now, why don't you scurry off and have some sherry, hmm?"

"Yes, yes, only if you think it best, Stefan. After all, you are betrothed." What she didn't know wouldn't kill her. With a satisfied huff, she patted his head — quite a feat considering the little woman had to nearly jump up to reach it — and closed the door for a second time.

Alone, completely alone with a woman.

Not that she was a relative stranger, but then again he had managed to shock her into sleep. How exactly he had managed to accomplish such a feat was beyond his comprehension.

Without much to do other than watch her, he took a seat on the sofa across from her and waited.

Time passed so slowly when there was nothing to do but wait. Looking away from her peaceful face, he did the only thing he could think of doing.

First he hummed.

Then he tired of his own voice, so he began counting.

But he was never one for mathematics.

So he braved another glance at the beauty before him.

And cursed.

How was it possible that he was betrothed? And to such a woman as this? Rosalind Hartwell! Was his father daft?

Stefan was unable to comprehend the turn of events since

his so-called death. It pained him to think that his family hadn't even tried to search for him! They simply took a sailor's word for it that the ship their son was on had wrecked, taking the cargo and all its passengers, save one measly sailor and himself, to the bottom of the cold blue sea.

And to return months later only to see that his brother had gone quite mad, and his father had lost complete control of the family. The only semblance of control it seemed he had was to pawn off the Marquess to the Hartwell family in hopes of an alliance.

The Hartwells and Hudsons went back over a hundred years. It was said that an heir must always marry into the Hartwell family, or some dreadful sort of curse would befall them.

Stefan hadn't been a good listener when his father spouted off about the odd family traditions.

After all, he had been too busy falling in love with his brother's wife.

He cursed again and shook his head. Maybe he should have stayed on the little island he shipwrecked on. Surely that would have been a more welcome environment. He had food, if one could call fish every day food. He had clothing, at least a ripped shirt and useless cravat. Oh, and he had companionship — that of a tiny squirrel who often fought with him over nuts and wild berries.

Woodland creatures. Yes, that's what he had when he was shipwrecked. Could it be that he was actually jealous of the woodland creatures and their easy life now that he was stuck in that blasted room with Rosalind Hartwell?

And why in the blazes did he continue to use her full name in his mind?

"Rosalind Hartwell," he tried it on his lips. Well dash it if it didn't feel good. But of course it would.

One more tiny glance, his brain told him. After all, for

some cursed reason, she was still sleeping.

He obliged himself.

Soft red hair crowned her head. Pale milky skin and a body that would make Isis green with envy. One thing was for certain, Rosalind Hartwell was a sight. And as much as it irked him, even when she snored, her lips looked beautiful, untouched, and begging to be bitten.

Bitten?

Perhaps he had malaria. Yes, that was it. He was ill. This was why he was thinking about biting, nay, *attacking* a sleeping woman.

Or maybe it was just because he hadn't been with a woman in...

Well, as previously noted, mathematics were not his strong suit.

"Mmmm." The beauty stirred. As did his blood.

Exactly what he needed at that point. Another reason to follow his more primal instincts.

"Mmmm," she moaned again, but her eyes were still closed, though now he noted that they seemed to move back and forth rapidly as if she was trying to blink, but her eye lids were too heavy to put forth the effort.

"Mmmm!" Louder this time.

Clenching his teeth, he managed not to choke, or swear, or think too many ungodly thoughts when the wench stretched her arms high above her head and yawned. Beautiful curves strained against the confines of her dress until the devil in him hoped they would pour over the dress, giving him adequate reason to be lusting after her as much as he already was.

"Where..." her deep voice spoke, eyes still closed.

He waited.

"Where am I?" She blinked several times, then looked directly at him and let out a scream so blood-curdling loud that he was sure his ears were bleeding with agony.

"Shhhh!" he put his hand over her mouth, which in hindsight probably wasn't the best of ideas considering she had just met him.

But her fear moved her. With a deft motion the chit sunk her teeth into his vulnerable hand. When he drew back in alarm, she elbowed him in the ribs and made an effort to elude him. He caught her around the waist and heaved her back into his lap in one smooth motion, holding her tight until she finally stopped struggling against him.

"Hello," he said, knowing it was the worst possible way to wake a well-bred lady — stare at her while she slept, scare her senseless, haul her into his lap, and offer an awkward greeting.

Savages, shipwrecks, and squirrels were looking better by the minute.

"Release me, you beast!"

"Promise not to bite, elbow, or scream? I'm not sure my ears can take another one of your screams. Perhaps we can come up with some sort of signal next time you feel the need to open your mouth?"

She began to squirm anew, making things all the more difficult for him, given his current state of… fascination with her body.

"My lady, cease your movements before I give you a true reason to scream." Stefan tightened his grip on her waist and slowly, effortlessly, bestowed a kiss on the exposed side of her neck. He told himself it was to scare her, and it was. Sort of.

The instant his lips touched her neck, she froze. He relinquished his hold and ever so deliberately planted her next to him on the sofa.

"I must say," Stefan adjusted his cravat. "That was a first for me. I imagine it isn't common for a woman to swoon into your arms so willingly."

Rosalind snorted and turned her brilliant green eyes onto him. "Surely you don't think it was your presence that caused my swooning? I was merely *hot*." She fanned her face with her hand as if needing to show him how sweltering it had been.

"Right," he said smugly. "And that explains how your body went completely rigid when you fell?" Did she think him an idiot?

Turning away she shrugged. "Are we going to discuss my swooning all night, or did you have other business with me?"

"Business?" He laughed. "I was in the middle of releasing you from the betrothal contract. So, yes. Let us call it business."

"And I believe I said, 'As you wish'."

"No, actually you said, 'As you wi—' and then promptly fell, quite wantonly into my arms. Since I am a gentleman, I've decided not to hold it against you."

Rosalind scooted away. "Are we finished here?"

Trying to mask the concern he felt, he replied, "Only if you assure me that you are in perfect health."

"Of course. I can't say I've ever swooned before. But I assure you I'm in perfect health! Good night, my lord." With a huff she pushed from the sofa, took two steps and began to fall once more.

Stefan cursed and caught her just before she hit the floor. "You do realize this is twice in one night. If I were one for happy endings, I'd say you just marked me as your long lost prince."

Rosalind glared, but was still somewhat paralyzed. She wished, in vain, that she could somehow communicate the scolding thoughts she was entertaining in that moment as she turned her glower onto his handsome face. And, saints alive, he was handsome! Truly, it was unfair to have only been betrothed to him for a measly few hours.

Was it so terrible to hope for a kiss from a man such as this? At least once before she died from this dreadful disease?

"Rosalind?" He brought his monstrous hand to her cheek, "I shall send for your carriage, you need to be put to bed."

"Yes, more sleep, why hadn't I thought of that?" she retorted, her voice thick with sarcasm. Her blasted legs were still unable to move, for they too had fallen asleep.

"Shall I carry you again?"

Why did she have to have so much pride? Begging her legs to work, she waited before finally responding with, "If you would be so kind."

His carrying her seemed effortless. And it was quite nice being in his arms, if only for just a few steps. At this angle, she could appreciate his strong jaw line, that of a Nordic god or a Roman gladiator. He seemed fit to kill first and ask questions later.

Unable to hold up her head any longer, she gave in to the temptation to lay it against his broad shoulder. He smelled of warm cinnamon spice and soap. Rosalind closed her eyes and took her fill of his smell, for it was unlike anything she had ever experienced.

It was then she noticed he had stopped walking.

"Why have we stopped?"

Chuckling, he looked down at her. "I wanted to give you a chance to take your fill before we went out into the night. There's no telling how much the putrid night air could take away my scent, you know."

Feeling the blood pound into her face, Rosalind hid deeper in the crook of his shoulder. "I was doing nothing of the sort."

He laughed. "So you say, Rose, so you say."

Snapping her attention in his direction, she controlled the urge to comment on his use of her nickname, one that only family used. The nerve.

The heaviness in her limbs began to lessen as he led her out the servants' entrance into the cool night air. Never had a spell come upon her so suddenly, and in the middle of a ball nonetheless!

At least she could be thankful that people were focused on Lord and Lady Rawlings as much as they were her — well, that and the sudden resurrection of the true Marquess of Whitmore. Curse him! Did that mean she had to call him that loathsome name? It left a terrible taste in her mouth, the thought of calling him Whitmore, as if he was even close to being as slimy as his younger brother.

Her fingers and toes tingled, the sensation gradually spreading to her arms and legs. Good. This was good. She could walk and wouldn't have to continue to be carried by the Nordic god who found nothing wrong with carrying her and touching her in the manner he was.

Goodness. She could feel... him.

They stopped. And how she hated to admit that the thought of getting into her carriage without the warmth of his body next to her made her a trifle sad and irritated that within their short knowledge of one another, he could make her feel such ridiculous emotions.

Well, he had released her from the contract, and now she was free to go to her estate in Sussex to suffer the fall and winter months without the city air threatening to burn her lungs.

"Rose?" He put her gently onto her feet, and only then did she notice that her skirts were billowed and wrinkled, giving him quite a scandalous view of her ankles.

Curse her body for experiencing a small thrill when his eyes lingered longer than was appropriate. *Take your fill — for this is the last you will see.*

"And here, I bid you goodnight." He steadied her on her

feet, then bowed gallantly in front of her before turning on his heel and leaving.

"Good night," Rosalind clenched her teeth as her eyes followed his disappearing form. The man was going back to the ball? Surely, he wanted to see to her safety? And make sure she made it home?

Was he whistling?

The shrill melody pierced the night sky. Apparently, he had much to be thrilled about. His betrothed hadn't held him to his contract, and he was back from the dead, ready to claim his throne and every other swooning woman in the London vicinity.

Gathering up her skirts, she launched herself into the carriage. Really, he was doing her a favor. Now she was free to seek out a man of her own choosing. A man who was tall, muscular, with beautiful eyes and—

"Drat!" Just because she had successfully described his every characteristic did not mean she wanted him. He was simply fresh in her memory. That was all! It had nothing to do with her desire, or anything else for that matter. What she needed, she thought as the carriage jolted, starting its short journey towards Mayfair, was to get away from London. Her best friend's marriage had done something to her; surely that was it. And the shock of not having to marry. And, well, her disease didn't help matters.

She had forgotten about that. How was she to explain that away to anyone who asked? For she was hardly the type of woman to swoon into a man's arms. Quite the opposite, in fact. Part of her brain, the sane and logical part, told her she should call on the doctor to see if it was worsening. The girlish fantastical side of her brain said everything was fine, and it was just a one-time incident.

As the carriage pulled up to her parents' home, she let out a sigh. Now that sleep was impossible for the next few hours, she might as well notify her father of the broken contract.

Rosalind steadied herself on the edge of the carriage and slowly put weight on one foot, and then the other. Careful not to take a misstep, she made her way to the front door and opened it, utterly exhausted by such effort for something so simple.

It seemed after every episode she was sluggish, her limbs unable to work properly.

With a sigh she looked up at the large mansion. Correction, the second largest mansion on Mayfair, for the first had always belonged to the Whitmore dynasty.

Taking a much needed calming breath, she opened the door and walked in. Her father, recluse that he was, was most likely in his study drinking tea — he had long since sworn off brandy — watching the flames dance in the fireplace for no other reason than he was slowly going mad with age. Or so he claimed whenever he was nagged by his wife, the current countess.

"Father?" She pushed the large oak door open. As expected he was sitting in his favorite chair facing the fireplace, but it was brandy swirling in his glass, not tea. Odd, she hadn't seen him drink in ages. He simply found it unnecessary in favor of a warm cup of tea.

"Ah, Rose," he said without turning around. "What brings you in to my study this time of night?"

"Boredom?" she offered, taking her favorite spot on the sofa across from him.

Her father, the Earl of Hariss, laughed. "You think me old enough not to notice the tone of your voice when you're jesting my girl? Now, tell me what has you returning so early from the Season's final ball?"

Truly, she didn't want to worry him, so she lied. "I swooned. It was quite hot after all."

"Swooned, you say? Rose, let us speak plainly, for I know better than anyone that you do not swoon, heat or no heat. That is rubbish, and you know it. I'm more likely to swoon than you!"

He had a point. Fumbling with her gloves she sighed. "I had an episode."

Her father darted up from his chair, brandy sloshing out of his glass onto the Persian rug. "An episode? At the ball? But I thought you were finally getting well — it's been weeks since the last one! The doctor said—"

"I know what the doctor said." Rosalind tensed. She hated doctors, for they could never figure out what was wrong with her. Instead they looked at her as some test subject to be pricked and prodded until she bled to death. "But it appears that the disease has not yet left my body."

"He assured me you were healed," her father stated. As if the mere pronouncement by the doctor that she was healed made it truth. In her opinion the doctor was a lunatic. For goodness sake, he used an incantation over her! Not that she would ever reveal that particular piece of information to her father. But the doctor, although he graduated at the top of his class and was known as the best in London, was quite odd. And at times he would stare at her when he thought she wasn't watching.

His last visit consisted of him speaking a spellbinding phrase over her body while she lay still on her bed. He then proceeded to scatter different herbs about her person and without warning announced she was healed.

"Just like that?" she had asked, skeptical.

"Of course! Am I not your doctor? Do you not trust me to see to your needs?"

Arrogant man that he was, she had merely nodded her head and mumbled under her breath the word "mad" while he went and announced the good news to her father.

The odd thing was she hadn't experienced an episode until tonight, when she saw... *him*.

"There is something else." She cleared her throat, waiting for her father to stop his fretting long enough to look her in the eyes.

"What is it, m'dear?"

Rosalind bit her lip in thought. Just how was she to announce the breach of contract? "It seems the Marquess of Whitmore is not dead."

The earl said nothing. Instead he stared for quite a long time into the fire before answering, "Are you certain?"

"Quite. Why he even spoke to me, and I can assure you he was no ghost." No, he was more firm and masculine than a mere ghost, with large muscles and a huge form, large enough to scare a man or woman.

Perplexed, her father stuck his tongue out in thought before sitting with a brooding expression. "And what did he say to you? I imagine he made quite a ruckus at the ball?"

Understatement of the Season. "You could say that, yes. However, I do have some good news. He has released me of the betrothal contract. However, I am not—"

Her speech stopped the minute her dad's face went pale with worry. His eyes closed, and he muttered a curse. "Tell me he did not break the contract. Tell me you are lying or jesting as you were with the swooning. Please tell me that, m'dear, tell me!" He launched himself from the chair and grabbed her shoulders, sweat poured from his brow. "Tell me, tell me!"

Frightened, Rosalind's voice shook. "Father, I thought you would be relieved, happy even! You owe that family nothing. Why, it's utter nonsense that we should hold true to that stupid rule about our families. There is no curse!"

Her father's head hung in defeat; his hands relaxed their hold on her shoulders. "What have you done?"

Those were the last words her father uttered before he

died.

CHAPTER ONE

Sleep hath its own world, A boundary between the things misnamed Death and existence: Sleep hath its own world, And a wide realm of wild reality, And dreams in their development have breath, And tears and tortures, and the touch of joy.
~ Lord Byron ~

Six cursed months later
"I REFUSE TO BELIEVE IT," Stefan muttered, keeping the tears from his eyes, though it was difficult considering the circumstances. But he needed to be strong for his family. At least what was left of it.

"It matters not what you choose to believe, it is a simple fact. Family members will continue to die unless you do something!" his mother yelled.

Frantically, he looked to his two brothers. The second oldest, James, utterly ruined for his stupidity, and the youngest Fitz, looking like he already had a foot in the grave. And all because of him.

His mother, the Dowager Duchess of Montmouth had

tear-stained cheeks. "Stefan, you are watching your entire family burn to the ground. Everything generations have built! Are you such a selfish ill-bred boy that you enjoy seeing the pain, my dear? For it will get worse. First your father, now Fitz. It is the curse, I tell you! And we won't be rid of it until you fix this!"

His mother spoke of the curse as if it was real. Which it wasn't. They didn't live in some fairy tale book where broken betrothal contracts made it so that people started dropping dead within the family until the contract was mended. His ancestors had been positively unhinged when they set about telling the family that they must always marry into the Hartwell line. Truthfully, he blamed his father's side of the family. Somewhere along the way, one of his ancestors had slept with a gypsy and then abandoned her, alone and pregnant, she did what any desperate woman would do.

She cursed his great, great grandfather as well as the woman he married, saying if he was so happy with another woman, his family would never break ties with hers. And so it was believed that if it happened, if either sides deterred from the chosen path, a curse so painful, so awful, would befall the family and take out all family lines and heirs.

It was ridiculous. But that didn't mean his father hadn't believed every word, nor his father before him. His family had promised he would look into the so called curse before Stefan left for India. Obviously he had come to the conclusion that things should stay as they were, for when he returned, it was to see himself betrothed. And the second he broke the betrothal, well, things had gone to Hades. His frustration mounting, all he could really do was explode with anger at his mother's refusal to listen.

"I do not believe in curses!" he yelled right back. If circumstances hadn't recently lent themselves in support of the family curse in the days since his broken betrothal, he wouldn't be having this conversation. But the evidence was undeniable.

First, Rosalind's father had dropped dead for no reason other than his heart stopped, yet he had been perfectly healthy until then. His own father, the late Duke of Montmouth, died two months later of pneumonia. And now Fitz, his brother, had contracted a disease that would not allow him to eat lest he throw up his countenance every time.

His mother said it was a curse.

He wanted to explain it away. For there had to be a more plausible reason why his once solid family was now crumbling around him, but it seemed too connected. Why hadn't he listened when his father spoke of such things? Instead he had thought them the ramblings of an old man, and even worse, he had laughed in his father's face when he warned Stefan to hold true to his promise to wed the girl, saying it was a life or death choice.

Apparently, he was spot on; Stefan just wasn't aware it was his own father's death that was held in the balance.

"What will you have me do?" He looked into his mother's tear-stained eyes. Willing her to stop crying — to stop yelling — he needed a stiff drink and some blasted answers, but knew he would only hear the mad ramblings of a crazy woman.

"Marry her."

A cynical laugh escaped before he could stop it. Taking a seat across from Fitz, he let slip an oath. "Just like that? You expect me to jump on my horse, tear after the girl in Sussex and convince her to marry me, all because of a run of bad luck which may or may not be the result of a curse?"

Straightening her back, his mother turned cold eyes on him. "How easily you forget. For wasn't she part of this whole debacle in the first place? Although, the rumor mill has been rampant that it isn't necessarily another family member who's struggling with life or death, but the girl herself."

"Rose is dying?" Stefan asked. His chest began to hurt. It felt that his mother had finally been able to reach him, for it seemed all the air in the once large room was sucked out and he now sat suffocating. His breath came in short gasps as he tried to regain some semblance of control over his physical reaction to the news.

"Very much so," his mother said. "And I'm sorry to be the one to tell you this, but from the sound of it, the girl doesn't have much time left."

"You swear it?" He had to ask it, for his mother was not above stretching the truth in order to get her way.

"Not that it matters, but yes. I swear it. Stefan, it was your father's last wish. His only wish, for us to continue aligning the families."

Suddenly exhausted, he allowed his body to fall back into the confines of the chair. "There has to be another explanation."

"But there isn't!" his mother snapped.

"She's right, Stefan." Fitz spoke up, his voice sounded weak with fever, it was strained, absolutely void of any luster. "You must do something."

Stefan looked into his brother's expressionless eyes, and his heart gave way again. How had things spiraled so far out of his control? And so fast?

"I'll leave as soon as I can," he said, looking down at the cold slate floor. It was, as he thought, a moment in time where he would always remember the look on everyone's face. His mother, in mourning and thinking nobody noticed as she continued to drink more and more sherry until her features took on a rosy appearance. And Fitz, silent as the grave, because even he knew he hadn't much time left.

The sunlight poured in through a crack in the drapes, tiny dust particles sprung to life all around Stefan's face, and it seemed the universe was frozen in place. His family utterly broken, silent, and grieving in that tiny death trap of a room. And he, the savior of him all, had just agreed to marry a girl with one foot in the grave. It was madness.

But it was also love. True love for his father who had died before his time, and his mother who was slowly dying every day, and Fitz. He owed it to Fitz for life had been the cruelest to him over the past few months.

Stefan had thought he was over Elaina. That hopefully through the passage of time, her beauty would cease to affect him.

Instead, he found it was worse. So when Fitz began his downward spiral into his sickness, Elaina had sought comfort elsewhere. The thought alone made Stefan ill, for Elaina had gone to James, of all people, for that comfort.

"How long shall it take?" James asked, breaking his sulky silence from the corner of the room. He was ruined more than anyone, for he had publicly announced a matron of the ton as his mistress, making him not only the laughingstock of the family, but also bitter for the woman who had denied him. Which was why he took his solace where he could find it — Elaina's bed.

"I'll be as quick about it as I can," Stefan said.

"Good," James excused himself from the room, not quite sure on his feet, for he had consumed nearly as much whiskey as his mother had sherry.

"Stefan?" With tremulous hands, his mother held out a crumpled piece of parchment. "It must be done this year or else…" Her weak voice trailed off.

"Or else?" Stefan asked, not sure he wanted to know the end of her tragic tale.

"The curse will take us all, Stefan."

Biting back another oath Stefan took the paper and stuffed it in his jacket pocket. "I'll return as soon as I am able."

"You cannot fail, my son."

His mother's last words haunted him as he quit the room. The only sounds in the depressed house were those of James' and Elaina's stolen laughter, Fitz and his coughing, and his mother weeping into her hands.

"I will not fail," he vowed, and went in search of his horse.

CHAPTER TWO

It is never too late to be what you might have been.
~ George Eliot ~

That same cursed day...

THE SNOW FELL THROUGHOUT the afternoon. Rosalind watched as the flakes danced through the darkening sky. The solitude in her hiding spot should feel lonely, but instead she relished the few silent moments to herself.

With her godmother running around the manor like a little mother hen, it was a shock she could even find a place to hide. Why, she had asked when she was little, did she need a godmother? Was having a full staff in the house not enough? Her father had merely patted her head and said she was extra special and in need of more than one guardian. Though her godmother scoffed at such an idea and swore up and down it was merely a precaution in case one of them died.

They believed Mary to be his insurance policy. But Rosalind knew better than that. Mary adored her, and she Mary. Since leaving her mother in London, her godmother was all she had. Her family had all but abandoned her since the night of her father's death, in hopes that the curse would follow only Rosalind.

"What have you done?" he had said. Shivering, she pulled her arms closer to her chest and sunk deeper into the chair.

"Rose!" Mary's high voice pierced the once silent afternoon. "Rose! I know you are hiding! Come here at once!"

Hide? From her godmother? Rosalind laughed. That was impossible, for Mary was everywhere every second, constantly watching Rosalind as if she were breakable. It was irritating to say the least.

"Here, I'm in here!" Rosalind yelled back, snapping the book in her lap closed. She straightened her shoulders and waited for the little woman's entrance.

Within minutes, Mary stomped into the room, face flushed with exertion. "Child! You simply cannot give me such a scare as to disappear for a few hours without a peep!"

"Peep," Rosalind offered with a devious smile.

Ignoring her, Mary marched towards the window where Rosalind sat. "Have you nothing better to do the day before your birthday than read?"

Rosalind stretched her hands over her head. "What would you have me do, Mary? It is snowing, after all. Would you like me to go for a ride out in the snow?"

"What a lovely idea! I'll tell the groom at once!"

With that Mary ran out of the room, yelling at the top of her lungs to ready Rosalind's horse.

She should have known better than suggest anything to Mary, the godmother who thought idle hands were the devil's playground. And that any person with enough time on their hands to sulk had adequate time to do something about it.

Legs heavy with sleep, she made her way up to her rooms to don a warm riding habit lined with fur and a muff. The last thing she wanted was to meet her death in the freezing snow the day before her nineteenth birthday. Her last one, according to all the best doctors in London.

Rosalind took her time descending the stairs, careful as she added weight to each step. She must be mad to go riding in such a condition, but part of her wondered if Mary wasn't just eager to get her out of the house. After all, she had been spending a record-breaking amount of time reading and gazing out the window. But her muscles were more fatigued now than ever. The woman, who was once fearless, was now full of fear. It seemed to choke the very life out of her.

The crisp winter air burned her nose. Though not extremely cold, it would most definitely be a frigid jaunt. Her legs continued to work properly as she made her way to the stables.

"And how is Duke today?" The smell of horses and sweat welcomed her as she noticed Duke already saddled and ready to go.

Hubert, her groom, laughed. "Aye, Miss, he's as feisty as ever. Careful out there, Miss. Duke is itching to go for a long run."

"We'll do fine, I'm sure." Closing her eyes, she ran her hand over his beautiful black coat, relishing in the warmth of his fur. Without assistance, she mounted and took off in a short trot.

Although she hated to admit it, Mary was right. The cool air invigorated her as the snow lightly fell around her, and absolute silence was her company — well, silence and the sound of birds singing and flying through the sky. How could everything around her seem so peaceful when war raged within her and her family?

The curse — it had caused all of this. And there was no way out, at least not according to her mother and two sisters.

So, she was not sent to Sussex for holiday. She was sent here to die. Away from her family, in hopes that the spell would lift once Rosalind paid the price of denying the demands of the family curse. Her sisters had argued against it, but it seemed her mother was slowly going mad since her father's death. In a way, Rosalind was the sacrifice her mother was all too willing to make in order to rid the family of the generational hex.

Was it really so wrong of her to want to marry for love? Had she known that decision would have cost her father his life, she would have run down the aisle, dragging that Nordic god kicking and screaming if need be.

But all hope was lost. It was the beginning of December, and if her mother's madness were any indication, the curse would lift only if Rosalind married before the end of the year. And not just to anyone. No, it had to be one of the late duke's sons. Last she heard, the youngest was ill with some sort of deadly disease, and the second oldest was utterly ruined. Rosalind's own mother wouldn't let her speak of him, let alone marry him, even if it meant the end of the curse. According to her mother, it would be better to die than be tied to such a man.

Leaving only the current Duke of Montmouth, *Stefan*. The rogue. If she closed her eyes she could still feel the warmth of his skin, and smell the spices on his jacket as he carried her through the thick night air.

Shuddering, she pushed the thought away. Surely, he had already found a more suitable bride. Looking around, she let out a large sigh. Nobody in sight.

It was safe to say that any sort of marriage for Rosalind was an impossibility. Not that it mattered, for the tonics had stopped working, her sickness was getting worse. Though nobody could explain it, the spells were less frequent but when they happened Rosalind had little control over her body in those times. What man would want to marry someone who was struck with sleeping spells? It seemed the only time she could sleep was when the spells hit her. To make matters worse, she had started to become somewhat of an insomniac at night, finally resorting to a family recipe for tea that was said to help her relax, though for some reason the recipe was safeguarded by the staff in London. She had sent a missive earlier in the week to obtain the recipe.

Lost in thought, she kicked her heels into Duke who bolted forward, sending her hat flying. Her hair, now released from the confines of its pins, spread wildly about her shoulders. Long locks of red whipped down her back as she galloped, small tendrils brushed across her cheek as the cold air stung her face. Laughter bubbled out of her as she urged Duke to go faster and faster.

"Ho." Pulling back on the reigns, she brought the horse to an abrupt stop at her favorite creek and jumped off. "Good boy, you liked that didn't you?" Duke neighed in response, his head bobbed up and down. She pulled an apple out of her satchel and shared it with him.

Humming, she closed her eyes. Allowing her daydreams to take hold. Her dreams were all she had, for she was plagued by them. She was constantly falling asleep. The spells would never last a long time, but dreams always accompanied them. Ones with dancing and laughter, bright colors and teasing. And always his face. It was the only face she continued to remember after she tried so hard to forget.

And always in her dreams, he would pick her up in his arms and carry her to the dance floor. Wrapping his large arms around her, he would dance and dance. The music never ended. And Rosalind would laugh in his arms, relishing the feel of his strength. Admiring the beauty of his perfectly sculpted face.

Lost in her fantasy, Rosalind curtsied, held out her hand, and began twirling in circles. Flurries of snow swirled about her feet as she flew around and around. She hummed and then began singing.

"Do you hear that, Samson?" Stefan slowed his horse to a walk as he listened to the air. A voice echoed through the skies. Though soft, it was so blasted alluring that for a moment, Stefan wondered if his mother's madness had caught up to him. Who would be out in this weather? And singing, nonetheless? Blindly, he led his horse in the direction of the heavenly music. As if sensing his urgency, Samsun trotted through the trees with ease, until they came up to a tiny creek.

"Hmm," Stefan said aloud. "Well, we'll just have to cross it. What do ya say, old boy? You up to it?"

The horse neighed in response. Carefully, Stefan guided the horse across the small stream. When they reached the other side, he dismounted and led Samson through the thick brush of trees.

"Have I found you? The one who makes me sing? Once upon a midnight dream..."

The voice haunted him, chilled him to his core, for he couldn't help but selfishly want this song to be about him. And the voice behind it. So clear, perfect. An angel from heaven.

Shocked about his physical reaction to something so simple, he cursed himself and moved closer towards the voice.

"As I lay me down to sleep, my midnight dream I know will keep. The stars in your eyes tell me what your heart is afraid to say. That while I wait for my prince, he will one day say..."

What urgency possessed him, Stefan did not know. All he knew was he needed to see the identity of this person. For his own sanity, he needed one glimpse. Starved, abandoning all sense, he finally reached the clearing. And swore.

It was her.

Lady Rosalind, dancing in reckless abandon, sans any sort of head covering. Her glorious red hair dangled past her waist. Her arms were held high above her head as she twirled and sang.

Stefan felt as if someone had punched him, and then added a heavy kick for good measure. Air, it seemed, whooshed out of his lungs; it was suddenly hard to breathe and difficult for him to do anything except stare, slack-jawed, at the most beautiful sight his eyes ever had the opportunity to behold.

Closer — his body demanded he draw closer. He inched forward and motioned for Samson to be quiet. So maybe he was a trifle mad. He hadn't been on that forsaken island that long; he knew horses could not speak. But he gave the signal, nonetheless, and dash it if that horse didn't seem to be tiptoeing just as Stefan was.

At the clearing, he stood only a few feet from her. A nervous chill ran down his spine as he fell into the hypnotic trance of her swaying hips. And then she curtsied. As if some other gentleman was dancing with her. Jealous rage poured out of him until he realized she was bowing to her horse.

At least they had that in common — both talking to their horses as if they were people. His mother would probably attribute that to the curse as well. Samson nudged him in response, and he lost his careful footing causing him to stumble. A branch snapped beneath his boot.

Lady Rosalind froze and ever so slowly turned to face him.

"Blast." He closed his eyes, willing himself to disappear; after all, he had just been caught staring at her like some daft fool.

"Your Grace?" Had her voice always been so husky, dripping with promises of seduction? His body warmed. "Is that you?"

Stefan stepped out of the shadows and into the blinding light of the clearing. He led Samson but kept his eyes focused on her. Not out of necessity or propriety, but because his eyes could do nothing else but stare. As if any other option was possible, considering the circumstances.

"My apologies, Lady Rosalind. I had no intention of spying. I heard your voice and followed." Like an idiot.

An amused laugh bubbled behind the woman's pouty pink lips. They were slightly parted, giving Stefan lustful thoughts about where he'd like to see that mouth placed. Those lips were created to give a man pleasure, to make him think about warm wet kisses and pleasures that he had no business to be entertaining. She shook her head. "Hmm, and how did you like the entertainment, Your Grace?"

He felt a slow seductive smile break across his face as he reached for her hand, his body again acting without his consent. Kneeling before her, he kissed her hand and rose. "The entertainments were delightful, though I was saddened to see you had no partner." He lied through his teeth; sadness had nothing to do with the emotions he was feeling at the moment. More like raw desire and jealousy.

Narrowing her eyes, she looked down at his hand, still holding hers.

"Dance with me." The words sounded so foreign that he thought surely he was losing his mind. For he had just asked Rosalind Hartwell to dance in the snow, without music, and only their two horses to keep them company.

An unreadable emotion flickered across her face. Clenching her other hand by her side, she seemed to be thinking, and then with a determined furrow of her brow, she brought her clenched hand away from her body and curtsied. "I would be honored, Your Grace."

And so it happened that Stefan experienced his first bout of laughter since his father's death. To think, all it took was a dance in the meadow with a goddess to restore him to his normal humor. If the London Society Papers could see him now, well he'd be shocked if Mrs. Peabody's quill wouldn't snap in half. Rosalind's warm hands seemed so small within his own. Though both were wearing gloves, he could have sworn he could feel her heartbeat through the thin kid gloves she wore. Stefan imagined her dainty hands, all feminine and frail as he clenched them within his own.

Pulling her into his large frame, he began to hum the same tune she had begun as he twirled her, only to bring her back in.

It was astonishing how his body reacted to this strange woman. Her hair tickled his nose as she leaned her head closer to his. Desire surged through him when she pulled back and licked her lips.

One kiss.

After all, wasn't he here to sweep her off her feet and marry her as soon as possible? As much as he wanted to believe the lie that a kiss would only serve the purpose of wooing, his heart clenched in his chest, his knees went a little weak, and he was sure the birds began singing. Slowly he tilted her chin up, giving him full view of her glorious alabaster skin and luscious bow shaped lips.

One kiss. His head descended. Their lips met. A sigh escaped from Lady Rosalind at the touch of their lips.

CHAPTER THREE

Who ever loved that loved not at first sight?
~ As You Like It — William Shakespeare ~

HER LIPS WERE MAGIC as they matched his. And when Stefan slipped his tongue past their barriers and tasted the sweetness of her mouth — he groaned in ecstasy. With a little sigh, she wrapped her arms around his neck giving him all the invitation he needed to pull her fully into his embrace.

It was then, with her soft body pressed so wondrously close to his that he remembered why he was here. Not, to his dismay, to kiss the girl upon their first meeting, but vie for her hand. For his father, for her father — but his brain couldn't grasp that concept, for he was enjoying this kiss too much. The tangling of tongues, the gasping for breath, the heady smell of desire, it was absolute magic.

Just one more, he told himself when he reluctantly pulled back and looked into her eyes, but he didn't have the chance. Samson nudged him in the back, quite hard, sending him and Lady Hartwell sailing to the ground... on top of Lady

Rosalind in the most inappropriate of manners.

"My apologies, I don't know what came over Samson," he said, holding his body over hers.

Lady Rosalind, with a mischievous glint in her eyes bit her lip. "Ah, so the duke apologizes for his horse but not his manners?"

"Manners?" he repeated, clueless.

Sighing, she pushed at Stefan's chest. "Not that I would expect anything more from a barbarian."

Taken back, he jumped to his feet and pulled her to a sitting position. "Barbarian? Are you addressing me as such?" What just happened? Were they not moments ago kissing and sharing an intimate embrace?

"Considering the only other living breathing things with us are our horses? Yes. You can safely assume I'm addressing you as such, Your Grace."

Irritated, Stefan wanted nothing more than to push the girl back down to her curvaceous bottom, but the gentleman in him won out, so he held out his hand to pull her to her feet. Once she was standing, he pulled her close, his body threatening a kiss as his mouth brushed tenderly across her jaw. Warm lips moved against her skin and whispered. "I would never apologize for something I did purposefully."

She swallowed and looked away. "What are you doing here?"

"I imagine you mean, here in this meadow, watching you?"

"Yes." Lady Rosalind cleared her throat and stepped around him to her horse. "Are you lost, Your Grace?"

"I hope so." He grinned. "I must admit if I am, I'm not entirely sure I'm ready to be found."

She laughed. "You rogue. Truly, do you need assistance back to the main road?"

"Ah, but what kind of gentleman would I be if I didn't

escort the lady home?"

"Your Grace." She mounted her horse. "Even I, being shut away in the country, am aware that your exploits are anything but gentlemanly."

He pulled on Samsun's reigns. "So you've inquired about me since our meeting at the ball?"

"Oh, news of your magnitude travels fast, even for a duke."

He continued to walk Samson in silence as she slowly rode her horse next to him.

"I am sorry to hear about your father's passing." Her words were almost too quiet to hear.

"And your father's. It seems a curse has fallen upon both our families, wouldn't you agree?"

He was testing her, trying to see if she believed in the curse just as much as his mother and family. For this to work, he needed her to believe in its importance. For time was limited.

As the snow drifted down around them, she urged her horse forward, the question unanswered still hung in the air between them, making it thick with tension.

"The curse," she said.

"I assume you know about it."

Nodding, she stopped her horse to look at Stefan. "I am aware."

Apparently that was all the information he was going to receive from her. They walked in silence the rest of the way to the house.

"Good day, Your Grace, and thank you for walking me home. As you can see, I haven't once fallen asleep in your presence, nor have I come to any harm. I trust you can see yourself out. The road," she gestured with a nod, "is just over that hill." Turning on her heel, she lifted her skirts to walk up the stairs. The girl sure didn't appear to be dying? Maybe his mother was mistaken; for the more primal parts of his body screamed that she was healthy — ripe for the taking. As unromantic as it sounded.

He waited and admitted to being transfixed. In all honesty, he was quite content to watch the slow sway of her hips as she ascended the stairs.

Smiling, he waited for the inevitable. At the top stairs, she paused, cleared her throat, and turned around. He waved, hoping for a reaction out of her.

"What are you still doing here?" Her voice sounded calm but did nothing to hide the tense jut of her chin.

Stefan laughed, loud and jolly. It felt good to laugh. And it seemed Lady Rosalind's every reaction made him feel a little less sad than before. "I thought that would be obvious. I'm here to rescue you." He made a gallant sweeping motion with his arm.

"From?" She put her hands on her hips in the most alluring way, drawing his eye to the spectacular cut of her Spencer jacket.

"Dragons? The evil godmother? Yourself? Take your pick, really. Or how about the curse that seems to be picking off our family members one by one."

She smirked and began descending the stairs.

"And how do you hope to fix this lovely spell?" Her eyes narrowed on him.

"We are to be married, of course."

Rosalind stopped walking, her once narrowed eyes widened in horror, and her face went a little white. Suffice to say, it was not the reaction he had hoped for. In fact, it was nothing close to what he had been dreaming nights previously. He could just see Lady Rosalind running into his arms, her soft lips against his, crying with relief over him saving her family. And in the end, him saving her from the terrible curse that seemed to plague them all.

"Absolutely not." She turned on her heel and went into the house, slamming the door behind her.

"Well, Samson, I think I could have done that better." He hit his gloves on his thigh and cursed. The horse nudged him in response and neighed, digging his hooves into the ground.

He swallowed his pride, because if he were being honest with himself, he had quite a lot of it to swallow, he took the steps two at a time and knocked on the door. No was not an option to either of them at this point, not when other lives hung in the balance. If need be, he would drag her kicking and screaming to the altar, witnesses and all. And when it was time to consummate the marriage, she would be screaming for other reasons entirely.

Stefan would start with her hair. Yes, her hair — letting it loose around her waist like the crowning glory it was. Then he would spend hours looking at her creamy white skin, fascinated with the glow of the candlelight upon it. Then when he could not bear it anymore, he would kiss every inch of that voluptuous body until she was panting — begging for more.

He raised his hand to knock again. She would marry him. It would just take more prodding than he originally thought. After all, he was a duke! What woman wouldn't jump at the chance to not only marry a duke, but save her family in the process? To say no was ungrateful, wasn't it?

He waited another few minutes and almost lost hope, when the door finally opened, and a short elderly woman looked at him with interest in her crystal blue eyes.

Her face was aged with wrinkles, her hair gray and pulled into a knot on her head. Though she was small, the gleam in her eye told him she could probably outsmart Samson and he both together. Regrettably, the courage given him by his own little day-dream spurred him towards more rakish behavior; he bent and kissed the woman on the hand, lingering as he did so.

Then things went horribly wrong. She kicked him in the shin because she was so blasted short. Then she cursed him for assaulting a woman in her own home. Add that to the already embarrassing state of arousal he felt after his vivid daydream about Lady Rosalind in his bed, and he was more mortified than he ever thought possible.

But things became worse when the woman, still yelping at the top of her lungs, pulled him by his jacket into the house and hit him across the thigh with her cane.

"What madness is this? Dear woman, cease your hitting at once!" He put his hands up in defense, which seemed to egg the lady on even more. Where was his good-for-nothing horse? "Samson! Help!" It was after that plea that he realized never had he been desperate enough in a fight to ask his horse to come to his aid.

Samson, however, did not come.

But Lady Rosalind did — slowly, around the corner — her eyes were twinkling with amusement. "Did you get him, Mary?

Get him? Was the girl implying he needed to be squashed like a bug beneath her boot?

"Aye, my lady, though the rascal pleaded for his horse to rescue him before I finished punishing him."

Lady Rosalind released a spurt of laughter before she covered her mouth with her hands, cleared her throat, and took on a solemn look. "Thank you, Mary. I am forever in your debt for welcoming his grace to Raven Court."

"It isn't polite to propose marriage to a woman after following her home, my lady, it really is not." Mary made a point to stare at Stefan longer than necessary, then raised her cane above her head again.

Stefan, quite alarmed let out a vivid curse, and backed away only to find that the woman was merely stretching her arms, as if the whole ordeal of attacking him had caused her muscles to be sore.

Feeling rather embarrassed, and for the first time in his life, horribly stupid, he waited for one of the mad females to say something — anything really. For he wasn't sure how to follow such an attack. A duke wasn't often welcomed in such a manner.

"Your Grace, dinner is served at eight o'clock sharp. If you are tardy, you will not eat, is that understood?"

When he didn't answer, the short elderly lady banged her cane dangerously close to his boot. "Well, are you mute? Or do you understand, young man? And for goodness sake, stand straight. You'll have a hump the size of London if you keep slouching." She continued muttering nonsense about dukes not knowing their place in the world as she shuffled off down the hallway.

And for the second time since meeting Lady Rosalind, Stefan was stunned into silence. Was nothing about this woman normal?

The silence was stifling, and he hated to admit that his breathing was anything but normal. But the woman had accosted him! With a cane! What man would be breathing normally?

"You're all mad!" he said, finally breaking the silence. "It's worse than I thought. The curse has reached the lot of you!"

"The curse? Oh no, Your Grace. That wasn't that dreadful spell. Just my godmother Mary, though I wouldn't take the chance of calling her cursed, lest she try to whoop on you again, and considering your horse is safely put away in our stables, You won't have anyone to call out to but me."

Irritated, he let out a bark of cynical laughter and gave her one his most rakish grins. "Are you saying you would not come to my rescue?"

Lady Rosalind mindlessly teased a piece of her hair that

had fallen across her cheek. "Curious, and I thought I was the one in need of rescuing? Porter, please show his grace to his rooms. Apparently, he is to be staying with us a while." Lady Rosalind smiled and again left him alone.

Nostrils flaring, Stefan called after her, "Does this mean you accept my proposal?"

That stopped her dead in her tracks. He watched as her entire body stiffened. Stefan waited for her to yell or at least respond in anger. Instead he noticed her body instantly relax as she called back to him without as much as a glance, "If that was a proposal, my heart bleeds for your idea of romance."

CHAPTER FOUR

*Love looks not with the eyes, but with the mind, And therefore is
winged Cupid painted blind.*
~ A Midsummer Night's Dream — William Shakespeare ~

ROSALIND KEPT HER POSTURE perfectly straight as she swept
from the room into the kitchen. Clenching her teeth, she
managed to hold in her scream until she calmly closed the
kitchen door, turned to face the cook and stomped her boot
into the ground, by then only letting out a tiny squeal.

Cook ignored her little episode as servants were taught to
ignore all oddities of the gentry.

The absolute nerve of the man! To think that he could
swoop in and propose to her without a care for her feelings!
Curse or no curse, it would be a cold day in Hades before she
made this little visit easy on him.

What was he thinking? That all he needed to do was
smile and wink? Was that all ladies in London needed before
they launched themselves into his very muscular arms?

She was no longer a debutante, and things had never

that easy. She would not stand idly by and pretend that all she needed was fake and pretty words from him in order to swoon as she did before. Not that she had actually swooned, rather she had fallen asleep in his presence, but he probably still thought it was the sudden sight of his beauty that set her off. When instead, it was her dreadful disease.

Her stomach grumbled. It was three hours until dinner, and her dancing and singing had her half-starved. Well, that and the kiss she had wantonly received in the heat of the moment.

A mistake she would not repeat. Ever. At least not today — tomorrow perhaps.

"Rosalind! Get a hold of yourself!" She chanted as she hit her fist against the wooden table in front of her. "You are a grown woman. You can handle a flirtation."

"But you don't have to make it easy on him — curse or no curse, my lady." Mary had entered the room, still carrying her cane. Not that she needed it, for she was a spry old thing.

"No." Rosalind smirked, gathering her strength for the onslaught of male beauty in the rooms above her. "I do not."

"We shall marry at once," the duke announced over dinner. It seemed he was not only lacking in romance but manners as well. They had sat in relative silence over the serving of the first course. Until, the unfortunate object of her disdain opened his mouth and announced their impending nuptials, in what had to be the second worst proposal ever to be heard. The first worst proposal had occurred only three hours prior, when the man had haughtily announced that exact same thing.

"Must women teach men everything?" She sent him a scalding look then lifted her napkin as if to instruct him how to use it. His barbaric face was clean-shaven, but covered in such a smug looking grin that she wanted to smack him.

Scowling, he wiped his face with his sleeve and continued to eat ravenously, much to Rosalind's dismay.

"Pardon my lack of etiquette, but before riding out to your estates, there was business I had to take care of. I took the liberty of obtaining a special license. As I said, we can be married at once. Forgive my haste in eating, it seems I was so overtaken with the thought of marrying you that I forwent my afternoon meal." He smirked, and with a wink, lifted more soup to his lips.

Closing her eyes, Rosalind tried to calm herself. She heard the barbarian curse as something hit the floor — her calming technique was not working. What type of women in London swooned over this man? Tales of his escapades had been the stuff of legends! The scandal sheets positively adored him! Even the most scandalous sheet of all, Mrs. Peabody's Society Papers, regaled him as a Nordic god come to save the women of London from pale and sickly English lords.

On cue, the barbarian dropped his spoon and let out another ear splitting curse, before looking up at her and winking. Yes, because apparently winking would cover a multitude of sins.

"Thirty seconds," she said, folding her hands into her lap.

"Pardon?"

Smiling, she answered ever so sweetly. "The time it takes to pick a flower for the woman you are courting."

"You assume too much! I know exactly how to court a wo—"

"Two minutes!" she interrupted. "The amount of time it should take for you to come up with a logical and romantic thought, beautiful enough to be made into a poem you can write for me."

He grimaced.

"My apologies," she added, cutting her meat. "It seems a brute like you may need far more time. Make that three minutes."

"Now see here—"

"Fifteen minutes!" Could she help that her voice was carrying from one end of the large dining hall to the other?

"Oh, I think I know what can be done in fifteen minutes." He winked again, ever so wickedly.

Pausing, she tilted her head, patronizing him just a bit. "Forgive me, Your Grace, but I doubt even your barbaric virility could last all of fifteen minutes. And I was alluding to the time it would take to accompany me on walk."

"Why walk when you can ride?" He offered her a juvenile grin before blowing her a kiss.

"Not what I meant, and please keep your crude humor to yourself. I'm afraid it falls on deaf ears when you share it aloud. Not to mention, I cannot take you seriously when you have split pea soup dripping from your chin."

Brooding, Stefan swore under his breath and threw his napkin onto his plate. He leaned back, crossing his large arms across his broad chest. "Are you sure you want to make this so difficult?"

Difficult? More like aggravating, irritating, and impossible. At her silence he added, "Rose... dear sweet, Rose. I can guarantee that you will be on the losing end of this little battle. Just imagine, within days not only will we be legally wed, but I'll be having my way with you every night. I find that my carnal tastes are even more awakened when I gaze upon that glorious red hair, imagining it pooling by your waist, covering your breasts in a most scandalous manner. Alas, that is only the imaginings of a man. I can only assume the real thing is even better. Shall we take a look?"

"Barbarian," Rosalind snapped, though inwardly she couldn't help her treacherous body as it warmed to the idea.

Liquid desire pooled in her belly as she thought about his large hands touching her bare skin, that sensual mouth bringing her to the brink of pleasure. Doing things she had only heard about but never experienced. "What makes you believe I'll even agree to this marriage? Your powers of persuasion are lacking, Your Grace. Why saddle myself to you when, according to your eloquent speech, I'm the stuff of dreams?"

The duke leaned forward, and candlelight bounced off of his high cheekbones. His eyes appeared black as he tilted his head to one side. "You will be my wife, Rose."

"Give me one good reason."

"The curse."

"That's it? That is your reason? No *I love you, Rose — You're beautiful, Rose*? Not even a *I'm so glad it's you the curse requires I marry, for my heart couldn't bear to be without you*?"

"You do realize you read too much, right?" At her grumbling response, he continued, "Love, is that your demand then? That I love you before I marry you?"

Rosalind looked away. How was she to answer that? Her heart screamed, "YES!" But, it was silly. How was he to fall in love with her in only a few weeks, and how could she tell him she would surely die early on in their marriage? But didn't she deserve, at least once, to be courted? To be wooed? Never had she had a chance. Not with all her betrothals. Sadly, her first kiss had been from the man sitting across from her. The same man who had soup on his chin and started proposals with, "We shall marry at once."

"Love." She heard her strong voice echo off the walls. "It is my only demand. You have to try, Your Grace. I am a woman. I wish to be pursued."

"And you think I have the ability to pursue you in the way you desire, Rose?"

Her eye scanned the man across from her. Every plane of

his face. The shadows that danced in the evening candlelight. The strong arms placed on either side of the table. His broad chest and easy manner. Not to mention his entire god-like presence. It also didn't hurt that every time she looked at his mouth all she could think about was his knee buckling kisses.

"Yes," she said more certain than previously. "I think you're up to the task. We have until the new year before the curse takes us all, correct?"

At his nod, she continued.

"I believe that will give you enough time."

"To woo?" His eyebrow rose.

"To woo and to make me believe that this will be the best idea for everyone involved. You have exactly twenty days before the new year, Your Grace. On the twentieth day, we will marry. If, and *only* if, you can prove yourself to be something other than the arrogant, spoiled, ill-mannered man sitting across from me now."

The duke leaned back in his chair. His body seemed too big for his seat. Suddenly nervous, she swallowed the fear in her throat.

"Shall we seal it with a kiss?" His loud chair scraped against the floor as he pushed it back and rose.

Rosalind felt her breath quicken as the sound of sure footsteps reached her ears.

"Your Grace, I—"

"Stefan. My name is Stefan." He stopped in front of her, but she was still facing the table; he was to her side. Maybe if she stood still enough he wouldn't make her do anything but be immobile.

"Rose?" He held out his large hand. An invitation, and not one of force or brute strength, but that of tenderness. Slowly, her gaze lifted to meet his. Stefan looked back at her through hooded eyes and smiled that devastating smile she had heard so much about. Deep inset dimples added a blindingly irritating sensuality to his smile. Straight white teeth glared against his still-tan skin. *Oh my, what have I gotten myself into this time?*

Rosalind pushed her chair away careful not to appear too eager to launch herself into his arms. Even as she rose to her full height, her chin still did not come up to his face, rather she received quite a view of his broad chest. The man was a giant, towering over her and everyone else he spoke to. Two of her could fit in his shadow.

"One kiss," he whispered, leaning towards her face. By the saints, the man was dangerous! At this distance, she could almost hear her own heart thudding in her chest. His soft lips inhaled and exhaled in such a slow erotic manner that she wondered for just an instant if he was using some sort of Hindu trance on her.

Stefan's breath was hot on her neck, and she hated herself for wanting to feel his lips again.

Eyes closed, she waited.

Stefan grabbed her hand. Her eyes flashed open, and she stared as he quirked a smile and bestowed a warm kiss on her hand, his tongue darting out ever so slightly to touch her flesh. The devil!

"I bid my lady, goodnight." He turned on his heel and sauntered out of the hall. Rosalind, continued to stand, and then swayed towards the table, bracing both of her hands in front of her. Legs like lead, she was suddenly fearful she was having another spell, but the feeling quickly dissipated, and in its place a funny feeling in her stomach. A fluttering of sorts. She closed her eyes and relived the almost kiss.

Curse the man for making her want him! Well, one thing was for certain. She wasn't going to make this easy. If he wanted a marriage, he better understand just what he was getting himself into. Rosalind had sworn to herself that she wouldn't crumble at the feet of any man. And she didn't plan on starting now, even if the curse was real, which she suspected it was, considering she had seen her father fall to his death with her own eyes. Something good had to come out of all the darkness that surrounded her. She just wasn't sure that the *something* she referred to was named Stefan. Maybe her curse was to be pursued by a man she could never truly have.

With one final glance around her, she sighed, trimmed the candles, and made her way to her bedroom. Tomorrow Stefan would begin his courting. She wondered if he even knew the meaning of the word. For although he had been home from India for months now, he still had the manners of a savage.

CHAPTER FIVE

How much do I love thee? Let me count the ways...
~ Elizabeth Browning ~

STEFAN MARCHED DOWN the long poorly lit hallway to his room and pulled open the door with more force than necessary. The girl wanted wooing? He smirked as he took a seat next to the roaring fire. Stefan rubbed his eyes with his hand and bit his lip in thought. It wasn't the idea, more the principal of the matter. Why spend time wooing when in the end they had to marry regardless of circumstances?

He sat in silence, as the options lay before him. He could either one, force her hand; or two, woo and hope she would come to her senses. What did he know about wooing anyway? It had never been necessary, and since his return from India, he had more trouble hiding from women then trying to pursue them. The trouble, it seemed, had begun when he made a complete spectacle of himself at the Season's last ball. Only to be glorified in the society papers the very next day by Mrs. Peabody — whoever she was, she obviously held him in high regard, for every single article mentioned him in some way or another.

His favorite meal always included boiled potatoes, which made every woman within his vicinity strike up a conversation about the stupid vegetable . He preferred a certain bay over every other horse which always led to women trying to talk with him about horseflesh, never a good idea when the women hadn't a clue as to what they were talking about. At one point a woman confused a Grey with the actual color and then proceeded to ask him why he preferred such a bland color instead of yellow or pink. Needless to say, he walked away quite frustrated. But the worst of Mrs. Peabody's crimes also happened to be a personal favorite. What his choice hair color would be on a woman. That very piece of information seemed harmless at the time, that is until he went to a small dinner gathering and noticed quite a few of women trying to powder their hair in order to gain the blonde hair color he so obviously adored. Never mind that women had stopped wearing hair powder years prior. Apparently it was to make a comeback. Not only did he sneeze each time a woman came near him that night, but one of the young ladies had an unfortunate accident leading to her hair being set on fire.

Whoever that deuced Mrs. Peabody was, his life had been absolute torture in the months following his return to polite society. It was no wonder his patience was wearing thin. Two beacons of society had fallen because of the curse, and now he was in the middle of nowhere trying to woo a woman who danced alone in meadows! Not that he should be casting disparagement upon her sanity, since only hours ago he had asked his horse for help.

By his weak calculations, he hadn't any time to lose. The girl wanted him to try and so he would, but if he failed...

"Blast," he said aloud. He could not fail — *would not* fail.

It wasn't an option for him to even consider.

Stefan heard his valet enter and rose from his seat. "Alfred?"

"Your Grace?" He made quick work pulling out Stefan's dressing gown and robe.

"Have you any expertise with women?"

Alfred paused his fingers on the soft silk of the dressing gown, seemingly frozen in place. "If this is about that godmother, my apologies for not warning you of her manner, sir. It is rumored that she's taken a mother hen approach to Lady Hartwell. If I had known she would strike you, I would have surely given you warning."

Stefan waved off his valet's excuse. "No, it isn't about the godmother, though I swear I saw my life flash before my eyes when she raised that blasted cane for the third time. I am inquiring so I may..." He lifted his eyes heavenward and took a deep breath to finish his sentence. "...Woo the girl," he finished quietly.

"You want to do what with the girl, sir?"

"Woo her," he said again.

Alfred stared at him long and hard. "Forgive me, Your Grace. Did you say you wish to woo her?"

"That is what I said." Though by the look of shock in his valet's eyes, he desperately wished he could take it back and forget the whole conversation ever took place.

"Woo." Alfred repeated.

"Yes, woo," Stefan confirmed, tiring of his valet's obvious amusement. He knew Alfred well enough to speak plainly to him, but he didn't expect him to find the whole situation so amusing.

"I believe ladies enjoy flowers, Your Grace." Alfred began helping Stefan undress. "There is also a rumor floating around in polite society that they enjoy amusing conversation and compliments."

"Stop mocking me, Alfred."

"As you wish, Your Grace." Alfred continued helping him undress until he was ready for bed. The silence was deafening.

Muttering an oath, Stefan looked back at Alfred. "Flowers, you say?" He scratched his head in thought. Whatever happened to women who were easily seduced by lust-filled looks and hasty advances? Oh yes, they were all back in London while he was trapped here in an ancient castle with nothing, save a spinster and Lady Rosalind to keep him company. He refused to count the servants, mainly because Alfred was putting him in a devilish bad mood.

"Would you like me to acquire some flowers for you, Your Grace? I believe I heard talk of a rose garden on the estate. Though in winter, I doubt any of them are in bloom. An orangery perhaps?"

Stefan thought on it. The last thing he needed was to propose with a bouquet of dead flowers in hand. Surely Rosalind would not find the irony at all funny. "No, Alfred. It is the lady's desire that I sweat and toil for her. Therefore, I will pick the flowers, sing the sonnets, go down on one knee and pour out my bleeding heart."

"Very good, Your Grace." Alfred smiled and bowed. "Will that be all?"

"Yes, by all means, leave me to my devices, so I can plan my seduction."

"Woo, sir."

Stefan paused. "What was that?"

"Woo," Alfred repeated. "To seduce implies you mean to cheat. To woo implies fair play where both parties are involved."

"*Goodnight,* Alfred." Stefan grumbled. He needed sleep if he was to start this little adventure on the morrow. The trouble was, he had never courted a lady before and hadn't a clue how to go about it. Flowers and compliments seemed to be forced. And with Rosalind's father dead, he hadn't a man to ask permission to court. It seemed he truly was left to his own devices, and he wasn't entirely certain that was a wise course of action. After all, he had only been back in London for six months, and during that time hadn't once pursued a woman. The last woman he had even thought about had been Elaina. But that was before the bitterness of her husband's illness and the loneliness of her bed changed her.

His father would not have been pleased by the turn of the events. It seemed the man knew what he was doing when he sent Stefan away, though he was the heir and titled son.

The idea jolted his memory. Lady Rosalind and her mother were obviously still living in their residences. Just whom had the title passed down to upon the late earl's death? He lay down and told himself to remember to ask Alfred in the morning.

Rosalind woke early the next morning after a fitful night of sleep. The only thing that sounded even minutely relaxing was a cup of hot tea in her father's old study.

It didn't help that it was her birthday today and nothing had changed. The snow still fell lightly over the estate, and the house seemed as glum as ever. She could only hope that the weather would let up enough for her to take another afternoon stroll. How depressing that the only entertainments to look forward to were walks in the cold dead snow. It could be worse, she scolded herself.

A loud knock came on the door, scaring her out of her wits. Before she had time to answer, it was forced open, revealing Stefan dressed and ready for battle. Or so it seemed, if the all too alert look in his eyes was any indication.

Swallowing the sudden nervousness at his presence, she rose from the desk and patted down her simple brown muslin dress and inclined her head to the side in question.

"Good morning, Rose. I trust you slept well." Stefan filled the large doorway, imposing his maleness into the dim room. The man had more confidence than the entirety of the ton combined.

Rosalind fought the onslaught of nerves and managed a small smile. "Thank you for asking, and yes I did. Is there something I can do for you, Your Grace?"

His only answer was the wolfish smile as he took a seat in one of the leather chairs. "Now that you mention it, I believe there are several things you can do for me, Rose." His eyes boldly scanned her from head to toe. "But more of that later. Alas, I must ask important questions first. To my deep regret, of course."

Rosalind did not like the sound of that, nor did she appreciate his obvious interest in her morning dress. She took a seat opposite him and forced herself to wear a bland expression despite the swell of nervousness she felt.

She leaned back against the chair as he leaned forward resting his forearms against his muscular legs. "I find myself curious as to who inherited the title after your father's passing? You have no brothers, so the only logical answer would be an uncle or perhaps a cousin?"

If only it were a cousin or uncle rather than the horrid stranger who not only held the title but the family wealth as well. She cleared her throat. "I believe the name he goes by is Dominique Maksylov, now the Earl of Hariss."

Stefan merely stared at her with a blank expression. "The Beast of Russia? The Russian royal, Dominique Maksylov?"

"So you know him." Rosalind winced against her better judgment. Clearing her throat, she managed to change the subject. The sooner Stefan left her room the better. "Is that all then, Your Grace?"

He didn't take the hint. "How in the blazes did that dirty Russian obtain an English title? The monster eats small children to break his fast!"

Rosalind lifted a brow. "In his defense, he is part English. His late father was a cousin to Alexander the first. I won't make the assumption that you know anything of history. He was the Czar. But I'm sure your education provided you at least that much knowledge. We are related to him through his English mother. Both his parents are deceased, leaving only Dominique. Considering my father had no brothers and the only male cousin now resides in America, the title then fell to our second cousin, the man I just named."

"Fascinating." Stefan leaned back in his chair. "You know he's known as the beast to every single person he meets in polite society? Can't imagine why the man would live in that foreign country with nothing but that blasted piano as his mistress. I'm sure he eats the souls of his tenants as well. Hats off, it seems you truly are cursed," Stefan said quite cheerfully, irritating her all the more with his presence.

Rosalind shifted uncomfortably; she was all too aware of the horrid stories about the man, and didn't need this savage to confirm her fears, least of all on her birthday! "I'm aware. Now if that is all you need, Your Grace, I do have some important things to attend to."

His lips curled into a smile. "My apologies, my lady. I hadn't any idea that you would be so busy with correspondence on your birthday."

Rosalind froze. How on earth did he know it was her birthday? Curse her enthusiasm that he actually paid attention to such details.

Stefan rose from his seat. "And here I was under the impression you should like to take a stroll through the snow and possibly partake in an indoor picnic with me. Pardon the intrusion."

He strode to the door.

"Wait!" she heard herself call. "Perhaps a walk would be agreeable." The last thing she wanted was to be cooped up pretending to write to family members whose only response of late had been to inquire if she had indeed broken the curse and married the brute opposite her.

"Agreeable or exciting?" he asked, not turning around. Her eyes greedily took in the vast expanse of his back. Strong, sinful shoulders filled out his jacket in a way that made her stomach flop. His hair was so unfashionably long! Leave it to him to make something unfashionable look so rakish and cunning. The temperature in the room took a considerable leap.

Grinding her teeth, she refused to answer, but merely folded her arms and waited for him to either relent or laugh.

He turned and looked directly in to her eyes. "Dress warm. The snow has let up, but it won't do for my future wife to catch a chill before our wedding."

Chill — she felt a chill all right. It started at her neck and slithered down to her toes at lightning speed. The man was too charming by half.

By the time she reached her bedroom to change, she had already talked herself out of the walk at least four times. Resigning herself to fate, she slipped on her walking boots and grabbed a warm cloak. Surely it couldn't be any colder than the day before.

Rosalind took her time making her way back down the stairs to a waiting Stefan. Things would be a lot easier if he were unfortunate to look at. Instead, his warm fur-lined jacket had him looking much like a royal prince.

He held out his hand but she walked right past him. She wasn't frail; she didn't need to be escorted through her own home, or even outside for that matter! Throwing open the door to the back garden, she took a step out and gasped. What once was only crisp harmless snow had melted and refroze into something quite treacherous. She tried to regain her footing, but felt her arms flailing about her.

And then strong male arms came around her, pulling her frantic body into a large muscular frame. "Maybe you should have accepted my help, hmm, princess?"

She couldn't very well jerk away from him unless she favored a bruised bum on her birthday. Tensing underneath his brace, she waited for him to release her. But he did nothing of the sort. Instead he continued to hold her against him as he guided her towards the safety of the plush snow.

"There," he said, releasing her.

"The orangery is j-just around the corner," she stuttered. And she somehow managed to walk in the correct direction and waited for him to fall in behind.

Stefan grinned as the girl marched through the snow as if nothing had happened. But she felt it, he knew, because he had felt it as well. The way her body felt against his was sinful and exhilarating. Like fire and ice. He obliged her and that insipid temper of hers, and felt the welcoming heat from the orangery as she let them both in.

The flowers were beautiful, all exotic in their colors and sorts. He found himself more entranced than he originally expected. But considering his only thoughts had been of Rosalind's proximity, it wasn't altogether shocking. Several lemon-colored flowers and small orange trees were lined against the furthest wall. Walking in the only direction that the rock path would take him, he furthered his investigation of Rosalind's favorite spot.

The heady smell of flowers and fruit penetrated his

senses. The alluring scent failed to alleviate the nerves he felt at the task at hand. How in tarnation was he to woo a woman who seemed to jerk every blasted time he touched her?

A brilliant plan began to form in his mind, and he plucked a flower, hoping he wouldn't be scolded, and then went in search of Rosalind, for she had suddenly disappeared ahead of him.

At the east end of the wall, Rosalind was leaning over a small plant. He stood behind her and slowly lifted the red flower and put it in her hair. She froze. He sent up a prayer that she was still breathing as his fingers fastened the flower behind her ear.

Her breathing turned ragged as his fingers brushed across her cheek. And then, he stepped back.

"Perfect," Stefan said, assessing his handiwork.

"Yes, well..." Rosalind touched the flower.

"Less than one minute, I believe." Stefan murmured.

Rosalind narrowed her eyes. "What do you mean?"

He reached for her hand and pressed a kiss to the inside of her wrist. "It seems you were wrong, Rose. It took me less than a minute to locate the perfect flower to enhance your beauty. Shall we see how many minutes it takes me to compose a sonnet?"

"No, truly, that's fine. I—"

"The red of the rose is a lover's hue, yet my eyes are besotted when I look at you. With skin so tender—" he reached out and cupped her chin "—and lips red as your namesake." His thumb traced her bottom lip. "I only ask that when you have it, my heart you will not break. Eyes of green, a tongue tipped with honey. Oh fair, fair maiden, in your arms I would stay, if only to gaze upon your face for a day."

Stefan's chest was heaving as he pulled her into his arms, laying claim to her lips. His need was great, but his desire to prove to her that he was more than a brute or savage was greater. Reluctantly, he pulled back and looked into her clear green eyes. "I believe I broke the time record on that one as well."

"Amazing," she said, quirking her brow.

"It was a good sonnet."

"Not the sonnet." She pushed past him. "Your ability to bring everything back to yourself. Mayhap the next time you write something so beautiful, it should be to a mirror that you recite it rather than a woman?"

With that she marched out of the orangery, leaving him again confused. Why the devil was she so angry?

Just as he was ready to swear aloud, she re-entered with a smile on her face. "And, Stefan?"

"Yes?" He would be lying if he said his heart didn't jump in his chest at the look on her face.

"That, was *not* a sonnet."

Biting back a string of expletives, his mouth dropped open as he watched her again leave him alone to his devices. Why the devil couldn't the girl be least bit encouraging?

Stefan trounced out of the orangery after her, purposefully making his steps loud and angry, quite like a young child who had just been scolded, but she had disappeared. He grumbled on his way to the stables to see how Samson was faring, slaying Rose the entire way.

At the stables, Samson was enjoying a handful of oats when Stefan strolled in. It was beyond Stefan how his horse managed to woo everyone within his vicinity. One time a patron of a store gave him apples merely because he thought the horse smiled at him.

Of all the ridiculous notions. Samson neighed and kicked his hooves.

"Alright, old boy, alright." Stefan laid his hands on either side of Samson's face and looked him in the eye. It was peculiar how well the horse seemed to read others.

"Blast, I'm going crazy!" Stefan muttered to himself as he grabbed another handful of oats and held them out to the horse who had become more of a friend than a mere pet.

"She hates me, Samson! Everything about me! I wrote a blasted sonnet, and she walked away! I guess maybe it could be that I keep kissing her..." Stefan began pacing in front of the horse's stall. "And maybe if I wasn't so pushy, she might actually wish to talk to me. But I can't help that every time I look at her I can think of nothing else except kissing her."

A branch cracked in the distance, putting an abrupt end to his blubbering idiocy. Frozen in place, he looked slightly from right to left before exhaling in relief.

The trouble with saying things out loud was someone might hear him. He glanced around the empty stable, then stepped back towards Samson and whispered, "And it's not that she hates it, Samson. Quite the opposite, in fact, if you get my meaning."

Samson looked at him without blinking as if to say, *"You do know that I'm a horse?"*

And then a thought occurred. It was an unfortunate truth, but a truth, nonetheless. The horse, it seemed, was better at courting than the master. How often had he been approached in Hyde Park? How often had women complimented his horseflesh? Women, who in his mind, wouldn't know how to purchase a good horse any more than they knew how to purchase Hessians.

"How do you do it, old boy?" Stefan ran his hand along the horse's glistening fur. "What are your secrets, hmm? A little neigh in the right direction and the ladies flock, isn't that right?" Stefan elbowed him, and let out a teasing laugh.

"Well, I must say this is another first, Stefan. Asking for seduction tips from your horse now are you? My, my, how the mighty have fallen." Rosalind quirked a smile as she approached Samson and nuzzled his neck. "At least you sought out a wise teacher. I'm sure he could teach you a few things, couldn't you, boy?"

Samson, the traitor, neighed in response, kicked his heel and smiled, yes it appeared that horses did in fact know how to smile, though Stefan could have sworn he was mocking him. Wanting to kick something, he managed to keep his voice even.

"Rosalind, were you wanting to go for a ride then?"

"No," her delicate hand rubbed the horse's shiny coat. "I came to relay a message to you. It seems you're needed in London."

"Reading my correspondence now, sweetheart?" Stefan swiped the letter from her hand and ripped it open.

"No, simply lying in wait for you to get summoned away."

Stefan grumbled a few French words under his breath as he ripped into the piece of paper. His eyes scanned the written words, but it was hard to believe that this piece of paper would be addressed to him instead of Rosalind, for it didn't concern him as much as it did her.

"It appears we are to be married today," he announced, handing the paper back to her.

"You jest. Enough with the horrid proposals. Are you truly leaving?"

Stefan reached out and cupped her chin. "Not without you, sweetheart. Your mother is ill and requires our presence immediately. And you are aware you cannot travel on your own without being ruined."

Rosalind's eyes widened. "I'll bring my godmother."

"Brilliant. She can sit between us and bring her cane." Stefan swore again. "We simply cannot bring your entire household!"

"We're not!" Rosalind clenched her fists and stood her ground. "I refuse to travel alone with you. We're bringing

Mary, and that's final! I won't be leg shackled to you against my will. Not now — not ever!"

"I did write you a sonnet…" Stefan said leaning in to kiss the fierceness from her face.

Rosalind licked her lips and turned away. "Sonnets are longer."

"Maybe I left out a few parts to keep you in suspense," he whispered against the back of her neck as he made quick movement to bring her back into his arms. He chuckled against her hair as he flipped her around to see him. His breath was inches from her lips.

She laughed. "Or maybe your brain couldn't handle so much information at once, and you ended it because you had no other option?" Rosalind's chest was rising and falling with great effort.

"I'm going to kiss you now."

"You wouldn't da—"

His lips devastated hers before she could finish her sentence. It was the type of kiss Stefan had always wanted to give, but never understood why, until this moment. It was aggressive, like all his kisses had been. But it seemed what he could not communicate with his words, he still wanted to communicate with his lips, in the most primal way he knew how. His tongue invaded her mouth, slowly at first, trying to taste what she lay so tempting before him. Rosalind's breath hitched as his hands reached around her, pulling her body flush against his. Her mouth was so sweet, so warm, it wasn't like anything he had ever tasted. It was fresh, invigorating, and it seemed the more he deepened the kiss, the more he felt he would never quench the thirst she had started within him.

Stefan desired to kiss her until she forgot her name, to arouse her until she was screaming for him to stop, and to make even his horse blush and turn away. Her lips pushed back against his, but it only spurred him on more — that is, until she bit his bottom lip. Yes, at first it was erotic, but when she did it again, and this time pushed against his chest, he relented. It was quite honestly one of the biggest regrets of his life, having to stop what felt so good to begin.

Laughing, he cradled her chin in his warm hand. "Must you always cheat? You never play fair, sweetheart."

"At least I'm playing, Your Grace."

Stunned into silence again. Wonderful. He stepped back from her as he tried to regain the upper hand. "Regardless of your feelings, my lady, we must be on our way first thing in the morning…"

Rosalind placed her hands on her hips and turned her head back towards the house letting out a puff of air. "Don't worry that ducal head of yours, Your Grace. I'll make sure I'm ready."

"Lovely. Then I take it you're still set on not getting married and taking the sorry excuse of a godmother with us?"

Rosalind reached out and touched his chest very lightly with her finger. He felt it all the way down to his… well, suffice to say he was quite wound up.

"You wouldn't be afraid of a little old lady, would you?"

"Course not, she's just irritating… and violent. You can't say she isn't violent. She did try caning me yesterday."

"She thought you were an intruder."

Stefan looked down at his expensive tailored clothing. "My apologies. I do look exactly like a ruffian."

Rosalind eyed him up and down. "Yes, you do. I am so thankful I am able to invite her to attend to me, for I can't imagine being stuck in a carriage with such a savage. Considering I have no weapons, her cane will be most welcome."

"Savage," Stefan repeated, lifting his lips into a tight smile. "Keep teasing me, my lady, and we'll see how much of the savage is still alive and well. Now, hurry on your way before, I forget my good manners and give you reason to need a weapon."

She poked him in the chest. "That may be a chance I'm willing to take..." she paused, inclining her head towards him.

Stefan's blood roared. He leaned forward, fully expecting to meet her lips. He closed his eyes, but felt nothing save her finger against his lips. "Perhaps another time, Your Grace. According to you, I have to pack. Alas, it seems our little tryst will have to wait."

Rosalind hopped off, leaving Stefan restless, wanting, and ready to bellow at the top of his lungs.

Samson neighed and shook his head. Always encouraging to be mocked by one's horse.

Stefan briefly contemplated shooting him, or at the very least, threatening to take away his entire storage of oats.

Instead he glared at his hairy mutinous friend and put his hands on his hips.

The horse was obviously not the least bit threatened and continued to neigh. Stefan huffed and stomped off.

CHAPTER SIX

To sleep perchance to dream...
~ Hamlet — William Shakespeare ~

ROSALIND LIFTED A SHAKY hand to her face. Truthfully, she was alarmed. Her mother hadn't been sick once that she could even remember. Whatever was wrong, it must be urgent for her to send for her. At any rate, it would be one of the longest journeys of her life considering she had to sit in such close proximity with that beast of a man.

She had Abigail pack what she needed and informed her godmother they would be making the trek back into the city the following morning. Mary didn't seem at all put out. Instead, she looked excited. So much for having a birthday celebration. With all her preparations for travel, it seemed her birthday would again be forgotten.

It was the same way last year. Rosalind hated that her little girl fantasies were still so present. Though she was old enough not to care about birthdays, it still made her heart drop to her feet whenever they were uneventful. Her father often told her that magic took place on birthdays — one just had to believe.

She believed, but the minute she opened her eyes for a miracle, Stefan showed up. He was not her knight in shining armor. Unless the knight was supposed to be egotistical and irritating, albeit handsome. The only thing that fit was the white horse, but that seemed too cliché.

Perhaps, the reason she enjoyed Stefan's kisses, or at least allowed herself to entertain them was because she knew her time was limited, and it was inevitable that she would die of this dreadful disease though she hadn't had a spell since retiring to the country, or at least that she could remember. Wasn't that a good sign? If she couldn't remember her last spell, perhaps it meant the disease was going away? Or maybe Stefan's kisses were just muddling her memory.

She should not have allowed him such liberties, but she seemed unable to control her more physical urges whenever he was around. It was as if his mere presence drew her into a spell that she was unable to fight.

"Cursed man," she muttered, taking one last look around her room. It was time to leave. Maybe in London she would be able to see Stefan in a different light. It raised Rosalind's hopes that somehow the arrogant man would grow or develop a romantic notion and pursue her like a man ought to.

A girl could hope. And it seemed hope was all she had to hang on to. That and the curse.

Stefan made his way back into the house slowly, taking in the expanse of the property. The vision in front of him was nothing short of extraordinary. Snow-filled forests swept out from behind the Tudor styled mansion framing the sight in such a picturesque view it nearly took his breath away. Such a shame that he wasn't to be staying longer. The adventurer in him wanted to see what else the lands beheld.

The wind picked up, nearly knocking his beaver hat to the ground. A chill unlike that of cold weather plagued him. Just as winter was enchanting the lands around him — and reminders of cold death lay in front of him, Stefan was again reminded of the seriousness of the situation. If he didn't marry Rosalind, and marry her soon — their families — both of them, would be doomed. It didn't matter that he wasn't convinced it was some sort of gypsy spell. What mattered was that he was given one way to fix everything. It was his fault that things had occurred as they had in the first place. Rosalind needed to marry him and if love was what she required, then his persuasion needed to be better than barking orders that they should marry in haste.

And it was for that reason alone — desperation and necessity that he went in search of Alfred. If he was to truly behave a gentleman, he needed some reminding in the art, for the girl was correct. His romancing was at a standstill, and it seemed that his only option at this point was to seek help — preferably from a human, not his horse.

Hanging his head in the only smidge of humility he possessed, Stefan went to his room. A knock soon came on the door. Fully expecting to see Alfred on the other side, Stefan blurted, "I need help!"

"I see you've swallowed that roguish pride of yours since the horse incident, hmm?" Rosalind winked.

May God have mercy.

"I was... talking to, er... myself." Stefan cleared his throat.

Red hair glistened as Rosalind wrapped it around her finger in thought. "First your horse and now yourself. Are you sure you're well, Your Grace? Shall I call for Mary to nurse you back to health until you're feeling more like yourself?"

"By all means, call your godmother. Perhaps she can beat the last of my pride out of me. Sounds lovely, I'll just be sitting over here waiting for the caning. I do hope she doesn't break it on my back when she lunges for my head."

"Oh posh. You're no fun whatsoever!"

Stefan's head perked up. Was she jesting? So, she did care. She—

"What woman beats a man who just sits there and mopes?"

Right. Stefan's mouth gaped open to speak or snap — really to respond in any manner, whether it be a grunt or some sort of beastly noise. Nothing came, and with that he did indeed find out that his pride was nearly gone. In its place was desperation for the redhead standing ever so provocatively against his bedpost. A few measly inches and he could have her on her back with that glorious red hair splayed across the satin sheets. His body hovering over hers, promises of pleasure and passion and...

"Your Grace? Did you hear me?"

He shook his head. Had Rosalind truly been talking that whole time?

"Course I did." Stefan cleared his throat. Saints have mercy on him if she asked any sort of repetition to what she just said. Curse his lust-filled thoughts!

"So would that be agreeable?"

Stefan nodded; it was really the only option he had at the moment. Well, that or lifting her skirts, and he figured one of those two options would probably result in him being on the other side of that blasted cane.

"Good! I'm so very relieved that it is settled! I do worry about this estate when I'm not here, and it would be so kind of you to help out."

"Help out?" he repeated. What in the blazes was she talking about?

"Yes." Rosalind winked. "I'll just let the estate manager know you'll be making the final preparations with him before we leave."

Devil take it, her smile sent tremors through his already hard body. "Yes, well, I would do anything for you, my Rose."

She lifted an eyebrow. "I can very well see that. Now, off you go. I'm sure you have much planning to do before we leave. I'll just leave you to your talking, perhaps looking in the mirror would help next time?"

"I was not — yes, perhaps." Stefan clenched his teeth and gave a curt bow as Rosalind's laughter echoed in the room.

"Until dinner, Your Grace. Remember. Eight o'clock sharp."

The door shut behind her, leaving Stefan with the aching suspicion that he had just agreed to do something horribly disagreeable. Well, he was a duke! As long as he wasn't mucking out stables and farming with the tenants, he would be fine.

"Son of a—"

"Oh, Your Grace! So glad to see you! We have been waiting in expectation for your grand tutelage!"

Oh, how he wished for his own cane, or possibly to wrap his hands around Rosalind's beautiful slender neck. Yes, he would cheerfully punish that woman for putting him in this predicament. Outside, in the snow, mucking stables. Dukes did not muck stables. Dukes rarely stepped foot inside stables unless it was to buy some greys or perhaps ride or...

"When you're ready, Your Grace." Higgins, the estate manager, was a short plump man with an all too cheerful demeanor and an aggravating voice that sounded quite like an animal in heat, though to be fair, worse comparisons were out there.

Stefan muttered a few more curses for good measure and plastered a ducal smile on his face while he reached out to shake the man's hand. "Higgins, it seems I'm a bit in the dark. Tell me how I can be of service."

"Right away, Your Grace! And may I just say, to work next to such a man! Well, I don't think my Betsy will believe me when I tell her!"

As long as Higgins didn't repeat all the curses Stefan muttered, repeating the story would be fine.

"Yes, good." Stefan looked around the stables. Where was all the help?

Higgins stepped closer to Stefan and whispered in that awful voice, "What'cha lookin' for, Your Grace?"

"Pride."

"What was that?"

Stefan cleared his throat. "People, my good man. Where are all the servants?"

Higgins brow furrowed, a bark of laughter escaped his lips. "Oh, apologies, I thought the lady of the house told ya. It's just me and the stable boy, cook, and of course, Abigail, and ol' cranky pants, the butler. We haven't had servants in this house since the earl's passing."

Which meant Stefan was to be a servant for the day. Oh the ways he would make Rosalind pay. On second thought... A smile spread across his lips.

"Very good!" Stefan slapped Higgins on the back and walked towards the shovels. "Shall we get to work then? It seems these stables need a good cleaning before we leave in the morning, wouldn't want the estate to fall into disarray with the lady's absence."

Higgins joined his side and slapped him on the back, obviously not aware that dukes did not, in fact, get slapped by servants or any person for that matter. But he meant it in good fun, so Stefan let it slide like he had so many other things the past few days — pride, sanity, good sense...

"Well, let's get to it, good man. Wouldn't want to keep you from Betsy."

Higgins grin was so wide, Stefan's own mouth grew slightly sore. "Thank you, Your Grace. I tell you it is an honor, it is."

"Right."

Stefan gripped the shovel. Rosalind had another thing coming if she thought he was to be scared off by a little work. Had she no idea what he was doing in India that entire time? Nor that his father had tenants and estates of his own before his passing? Ones that Stefan saw flourish under his own two bare hands. If she wanted help, well, help was what she would get.

And with that, Stefan began to whistle a tune.

CHAPTER SEVEN

Hear my soul speak;
The very instant that I saw you, did
My heart fly to your service.
~ The Tempest — William Shakespeare ~

ROSALIND LOOKED OUT THE window facing the stables and froze. Was that...? Her ears strained to hear the melodious tune. No, it couldn't be. The man was whistling! And the blasted horses seemed to be dancing along with that sorry tune.

"Of all the..." Her eyes flashed back to the window. Breath stole straight out of her lungs causing her to choke. The duke had removed his jacket. Seconds later, his shirtsleeves, as he began the laborious chore of chopping wood. May God rain curses on him for being such a fine specimen to look at.

Her elbows leaned on the windowsill of their own accord; her chin soon followed until she was leaning against the window, pasting her face to the glass so hard her nose was smooshed.

"My Lady?" A man's voice penetrated her spying, throwing cold water onto the fervor of heat. With a bang, her forehead hit the window. Rolling her eyes, she put a hand to her skin hoping it wouldn't bruise and turned around.

"Yes, Alfred?"

"I merely came to see if you needed any more assistance, were the windows dirty? Perhaps a good cleaning before we off tomorrow?" Alfred made a move to look out the window.

"No!" Rosalind yelled pressing her hands against the valet's chest. With a jerk she pulled them back and let out an embarrassed laugh. "I mean, no need! I was just inspecting them for dust and they seem to be perfect. Not one speck of dust, or fat, or deformity..."

Alfred turned his head to the side in thought. "On the windows, you say?"

"Course, yes. I meant the windows, whom, I mean what else would I be referring to?" She nervously cleared her throat and clenched her hands behind her back.

"Right then. I shall sleep soundly tonight knowing there isn't at trace of fat on them. Good day, miss." Alfred gave her a knowing wink, then walked off just as another hot wave of embarrassment washed over her.

Sighing, she turned back towards the window. Just one more glance, she told herself as her eyes searched for Stefan's muscled form. Where the devil did he go? Rosalind pressed her nose closer, her eyes now roaming in earnest to search the estate grounds.

"What are we looking for?" Stefan's breath fanned the side of her neck making the embarrassment complete.

"Ah, Your Grace! Was just looking for you. It seems the windows are clean!" Alfred announced coming back in their direction.

Oh no.

"Is that so?" Stefan said still standing dangerously close

to Rosalind who had yet to take her eyes off the cursed window.

"Oh yes, miss Rosalind was very perceptive earlier when she was looking at them for all traces of… Let me see what did you say? Oh yes dust and fat, was it, Miss?"

"What is this nonsense?" Mary walked up behind Alfred. "We do not use fat to wash our windows!"

"Did you need something, Mary?" Rosalind nearly yelled above the commotion.

"Yes, Cook isn't yet back with supplies and we need all the help we can get in the kitchens."

Rosalind smiled, feeling the upper hand. "I'll just send His Grace down in a bit, shall I?"

"Very good!" Mary stomped her cane and walked off. Rosalind allowed herself a brief smile. She would like to think that every time Mary came into the room Stefan was a trifle fearful of the cane she carried.

"But—" Stefan opened his mouth to say more, but Rosalind took advantage of his being tired from hours of work.

"No buts, Your Grace. You said you'd help in any capacity, it seems we are to help with dinner tonight. That is, if you don't mind getting your ducal hands a bit dirty."

Stefan leaned in pinning her against the wall and his rock hard body. "I think we both know I don't mind a bit of dirt." His eyes locked on her lips, and instinctively she leaned in.

Alfred coughed.

With a shaky hand, Rosalind pushed Stefan back, so what if that same hand stayed longer than necessary across the flat planes of his godlike stomach? He was solid, hard, and so foreign, yet her hand remained, until Stefan cleared his throat. Pulling back as if burned, she snapped a retort, "I'll see you after you clean up a bit, Your Grace."

On wobbly legs, she made her exit and prayed the entire

way that God would grant her momentary blindness so she wouldn't fall into the wicked temptation pooling in her mind.

CHAPTER EIGHT

Smiles form the channels of a future tear.
~ Lord Byron ~

THE LARGE KITCHEN WAS a sight to behold, even for Rosalind. Alfred was in the corner learning the proper practice in making bread. Mary was working at the stove stirring the stew, and to Rosalind's amusement, Stefan was to cut vegetables for the dinner.

Not that anyone would point it out, but the duke wasn't exactly skilled in the kitchen. The stew hadn't been the first choice, but after nearly setting his valet as well as the rest of the kitchen on fire, it was decided that his certain talents would make an excellent stew. So he sat, in the corner, much like a punished young boy and peeled carrots and potatoes.

"Missed one." Rosalind couldn't help it. With a little push, she put the potato in front of the duke. Probably not her smartest moment considering the knife he held was quite menacing. It had a large serrated blade, and in his more than capable hands, it looked more like a sword.

Stefan glared at the missed potato, but instead of snapping at her, he smiled a sinfully sweet smile and peeled the potato without complaining, whistling that same blasted tune he'd been whistling upon their first meeting.

It was difficult not to tease the man. His presence alone filled up half the kitchen, then to see the tiny vegetables in his hands; it was too much to take in. Rosalind had to continuously cough in order to hide her laugh. Serves him right for not listening to her earlier that day when she asked how long the trip would be.

Instead of answering, he had given her one of those wicked smiles and looked at the bed as if he meant to take her right then and there. It wasn't at all shocking that he had missed her simple question. So what if she tricked him into thinking he had agreed to help around the manor? They did need help as short staffed as they were.

Rosalind just wasn't counting on Stefan being such a big help, nor her estate manager, tears in his eyes, offering to erect a statue in his honor. Wouldn't surprise her one bit if he already wrote a song about the duke.

"Ah, smells good! Oh, looky at all ya fancy folk in here workin' in the heat. Dear me. Well, I'm back now, so off with you!" Cook shooed them out of the kitchen quicker than a hound on the hunt.

Alfred, Mary, Stefan, and Rosalind watched as the doors closed behind them. They still had a few hours before the night time meal. With a thump, Mary's cane came crushing down onto the floor.

"Well it's back to work for me. Want to make that birthday special for ya, since this one burnt the first pie. I'll just think of something else then." Mary pointed at Stefan and pushed back into the kitchen.

"Sorry I burnt the pie." Stefan hung his head. "In my defense, I was so concerned about the flying cane in the kitchen that I wasn't concentrating on anything that witch said."

"Flying canes are indeed dangerous, Your Grace." Alfred nodded his head somberly. Rosalind covered her laughter with the back of her hand.

"Anything else, Rose?" Stefan turned his full body towards her, again pinning her against the wall and blocking her only escape route.

Alfred cleared his throat. "With your permission, sir I'll just—"

"Go away, Alfred."

"Very good, Your Grace."

Rosalind glared after his retreating form. The traitor should at least chaperone his brute of a master.

"He's not coming back." Stefan read her thoughts as he leaned in closer, she could smell the sweat right off his skin. "Nobody to guard your virtue anymore, eh Rose?"

Rosalind scoffed. "Guard my virtue? I wasn't at all concerned, Your Grace."

Stefan's smile curled upwards towards his eyes. Tiny crinkles paraded around his piercing gaze as he leaned even closer. Shudders of excitement traveled down Rosalind's body as his look went from hungry to ravenous. Lifting his hand he traced the line of her jaw with his finger using only the slightest of pressure. Trembling under his touch, Rosalind could only close her eyes against the god-like man standing in front of her.

"No, Rose, you may not close your eyes. You may not escape me. Not after putting me through such a toil-filled day. I imagine you meant to punish me or to at least intimidate me. Perhaps scare me off?"

What could she do but nod and pray his lingering would cease?

"I was shipwrecked."

Everyone knew he was shipwrecked. Was his purpose now to gain her pity? "Yes, I know." Rosalind's voice shook.

"I built fires."

Well if praise was what he wanted. "How very brave, Your Grace."

"Stefan," he corrected with a wink. "Thank you, but I was not looking to obtain favor. Do you know what it is like to be shipwrecked? To think yourself dead? To hunt for food and make shelter? How about owning more than ten estates, each with tenants who depend solely on you for their next meal. You've shown me your life, Rose, but you've left me to wonder, do you know my reality?"

Sheepishly, she shook her head, suddenly embarrassed that she would think him like every other duke of the realm. A duke who would never toil along with other workers, and sweat with the common man. A duke who would rather spit on work than lift one soft finger.

"I-I was not aware… Stefan." She lifted her head. "But we did need help, we *do* need help! We are short staffed and everyone pulls their weight around here. I meant not to punish you merely to teach you a lesson, for your forwardness."

"So we get to the bones of it don't we, sweetheart?"

"I know not what you mean." Oh sweet deliverance, if only she could inch by him and run up the stairs. They called to her — escape called to her.

"Think it is I who will teach you a lesson, my dear."

And with that Stefan's head descended towards her lips. He let out a throaty chuckle as his lips rained kisses up her neck, stopping just once near her ear, pulling it between his teeth. Gooseflesh rose all over her arms as she felt his breath caress her neck. The sweetness of his proximity threatened to overwhelm her as his skin, just slightly in need of a good shave, rubbed against her cheek.

Warm strong hands cupped her face drawing her lips dangerously close to where his hovered. With a mind of its own, her body leaned towards him, nearly shaking with excitement. Surely he was hypnotizing her!

Cautiously, his warm lips moved to kiss each cheek, and then her forehead, her nose, her eyelids. He was trying to drive her mad! Stefan paused the onslaught of seduction and pulled away.

Embarrassed, Rosalind's eyelids flew open to see a smug grin spread across Stefan's face.

"Lesson one," he said.

"Lesson one?" Rosalind repeated voice shaky, her entire body buzzed with excitement and need. The only thing keeping her upright was Stefan's muscular body holding her firm against the wall.

"Always leave with your opponent begging for more."

"I do not—"

"—Lesson two. Start with a simple caress or touch." His hands again reached out and cupped her face before his thumb rubbed across her bottom lip, finally dipping into her mouth just slightly before he said, "And lesson three."

Rosalind swayed on her feet as Stefan lifted his body away from hers. "What is lesson three?"

"Tonight, Rose. I'll show you tonight."

With a bow, Stefan took his leave and marched up the stairs, leaving Rosalind so bewildered she wasn't sure in which direction to go. So instead of walking anywhere, she slowly slid down the wall and sat in the middle of the hall and pulled her knees to her chest. Stefan's familiar whistle reached her ears. As she fought to keep herself from smiling, she realized that for once in her life she had been thoroughly bested.

Rosalind's shaky legs took her down the staircase towards the dining room. Curse that arrogant man for making her feel so weak! She would not — no she *could* not allow him to have such power over her! She hadn't expected the man to be so open to manual labor, nor for his countenance to be that of a thankful servant instead of a boastful duke. Why, she was even told by the stable hand that he helped birth a cow! Perhaps he was putting on a show for her? Logically, it would make sense, but she knew in her soul the man who constantly whistled — who talked to his horse like a fellow man — this was the true duke. And the more she thought on it, the more uncomfortable she became.

The very idea that he was pulling down her defenses was unnerving, not to mention that he thought to teach her yet another lesson.

Lesson one and two were hard enough, and her virgin mind could only horrifyingly bring up images of what his version of lesson three might be! With a deep breath, she entered the large dining room and gasped.

Stefan was standing next to her chair. The fire roared next to the table, but it wasn't heat she felt, but gooseflesh all over her body. For the barbarian of a man had cleaned up quite nicely. Blond hair was tucked behind his ears, his boots shined to perfection, and his dinner jacket hugged his large frame perfectly. His glaring white teeth against tanned skin were devastating, and for once in her life Rosalind thought she might actually swoon for want. Lustful desire made her knees weak as she continued to stare at the man. Her own body physically responding as her breathing hitched, and a throbbing ache made it's presence known. Her heart didn't help the matter for it thudded helplessly against her chest, "this one," it said over and over again. Stefan's chest rose and fell in cadence with Rosalind's own heartbeat. It seemed to take an eternity as she walked to where he stood and did a slow curtsy.

"No," Stefan murmured lifting her chin up with his gloved finger. "It is I who will bow to you, for the birthday girl should never have to humble herself or have proper manners on such a day."

Lifting a rakish brow, he bowed crisply, beautifully in front of her, his entire presence leaning ever so slightly in the air and returning back to his full stance. And then with the grace of hundreds of years of breeding helped her to her seat but not before bestowing a kiss upon her hand.

"*My* lady," His words lingered on the word *my* — warmth radiated through Rosalind's body until she thought she may promptly faint out of her seat as he took a chair next to her.

"Are you well?" Stefan asked.

"What? Yes?" Rosalind answered the affirmative; in all honesty, her eyes had been so thoroughly trained on his broad shoulders that she hadn't heard a thing. Ironic, since she had punished him earlier today for being guilty of a similar crime.

Feeling her cheeks flush with embarrassment, Rosalind looked down at the table. The need to escape and break the spell he so powerfully wielded over her was almost suffocating.

"Hmm, it seems my punishment is appropriate then."

"Whatever do you mean?" Rosalind feigned a weak smile and took a sip of wine. There wasn't enough wine in all of Europe to make her nerves wither away. Why hadn't she taken to brandy?

"I mean—" Stefan said as he moved to his seat closer to hers. Lovely. They were apparently dining casual. At this rate, he would have her jumping over the table just to get the madness over with. Perhaps a chandelier would fall on her head? "—that you punished me soundly, or so you thought, for not paying attention to you when you were speaking. Alas, can you blame me, sweet Rose? For I was imagining how my hands would feel all over your body. How the nectar of your mouth would taste... I imagine you were thinking similar things when you entered the room, and by the blush on your cheeks, I can see that I'm right. So, truly, it is only fair, sweetheart."

"Fair, hah!" Rosalind reached for her wine again, but Stefan pushed it out of her reach.

"*Tsk, tsk*, wouldn't want you to be foxed during the lesson."

The man had a point. No telling how many liberties she would allow him when she wasn't in her right mind.

With a sigh, she leaned back against the firm chair. "So, this lesson, is it starting now?"

His rich laughter filled the room. Excitement jumped through her. "Believe me, Rose. You shall know when the lesson is to start."

With that, cook and Mary brought out the food. Stefan was wonderful conversation, telling her tales of his life in India. And Rosalind found herself wanting nothing more than to relax in his presence, but every so often he would smile and the candlelight would catch on his face. Or his leg would somehow manage to touch hers. And once, he leaned over and wiped a bit of desert from her face. She could have died from lust-filled mortification. In fact, it wouldn't have surprised her at all if she would have exploded.

But it was as if he wasn't affected at all! He just continued to relax and tell stories as if it was the most natural thing ever to be so familiar with her. It was driving her mad. She wasn't sure how much longer she could take it.

"And then," Stefan said scooting his chair closer. "Banana ran into the maharajahs tent and stole as many pieces of fruit as his little hands could carry. He took all types of fruit.

Apples, oranges, pomegranates. Say, have you had a pomegranate before?"

"No." Considering Rosalind's wine was being monitored by Stefan, she took only a sip and waited.

Stefan grinned and leaned in. She could smell the wine on his breath as he continued his tale. "They say pomegranates are the fruit of love. I say it's the fruit of lust. You see they have these tiny seeds." He reached out for her hand and opened it in his. "You put them in your hand like this, as many as you can and then you eat them. Each seed has its own delicious flavor that pops in your mouth. It quite makes my mouth water when I think on that delicious flavor rolling around my tongue."

Rosalind let out a sigh, as Stefan pulled her out of her chair and flush against his body.

Ripe. She was ripe for him. Wanting him, needing him. Any more innuendos and she would freely ruin herself just for a taste of his exotic kiss.

"Lesson three," Stefan's lips said against Rosalind's.

"What's lesson three?"

His warm breath tangled with hers as his lips just barely touched onto hers. His teeth tugged her bottom lip as he nibbled.

"Mmm, better than pomegranates," he murmured against her lips again. "Now off to bed with you."

In a daze, Rosalind shook her head. "What? I don't understand, what's lesson three?" And why was her cursed body shaking so much?

Stefan laughed and looked to the ceiling. "Unsated desire, my dear. That shall be your third and final lesson for the night. Sweet dreams, my Rose."

Curse words that she only heard mumbled by the servants and her father blared like a horn in her head.

She couldn't very well kiss him! That would mean he was

winning during this whole wooing business! But in her current state? Well, in her current state, she was already imagining what his skin would feel like against hers.

"Fine." Voice shaky, she did a small curtsy and nearly tripped on her skirts as she ran up the stairs and slammed the door. So much for trying to have a good night's sleep. What she wouldn't give for one of those sleeping spells now!

Stefan swore good and hard and pushed a chair. He tried roaring a bit but didn't want to frighten cook or Mary who were just in the next room enjoying their food. Nor was he inclined for Mary to think he was some sort of beast tearing apart the tapestries, making her feel the need to run in with cane raised high above her head like a savage.

What in the blazes had he been thinking? Torture her and then leave himself with such aroused need that he was ready to run around in the snow without clothes just to alleviate the pain.

"Well, that was brilliant," he mumbled to himself.

"What was that, Your Grace?" Alfred entered the room.

Ah, perfect, a friend to play with in Hades. "Nothing, Alfred. We leave tomorrow."

"Very good, Your Grace." Alfred bowed to take his leave.

"Alfred?" Stefan asked without turning around.

"Yes, Your Grace?"

"What do women like for their birthdays?"

Alfred cleared his throat. "I overheard cook talking about the lady's delight for fairy cakes, Your Grace."

"That will be all, Alfred."

"Yes, Your Grace."

Perfect. The one desert he could imagine bringing to the bedroom and licking off of her. Would his torture know no end? His body screamed at him, demanding that he go possess the girl. He made his way slowly up the stairs. Oh, she would get fairy cakes and a lot more if he had something to say about it.

CHAPTER NINE

All days are nights to see till I see thee,
And night's bright days when dreams do show me thee
~ Sonnet 43 — William Shakespeare ~

ROSALIND DECIDED IT WOULD be best to sit opposite Stefan and use Mary as a buffer. She needed a reason to stop his advances and could think of no one else up for the job but Mary, who indeed thought it best to bring her weapon along. Smiling to herself as Stefan looked at the arrangements, she gave him a little nod as he lifted himself up into the carriage. His body seemed to fill the entire side. And Rosalind immediately realized her mistake, for even across from him, his legs could easily brush against hers when outstretched. She found herself looking around for way to make herself smaller so she wouldn't somehow find herself touching him. Eyes darting around, she finally gave up and squished herself into the corner. She didn't need any more lessons from him.

Mary was perfectly happy sitting next to her if her smug grin was any indicator of her inner thoughts. The carriage slowly rocked forward and Rosalind found herself sighing in relief. The sooner they left, the sooner they got there and she could be away from Stefan's brooding glare and all too excitable kisses.

The groom was only too happy to ride Samson as Stefan relinquished his hold on the horse and decided to ride in the carriage. Rosalind knew it was to vex her. It had to be.

The carriage hit a bump and she scrambled to grab the seat so she wouldn't go sailing into his arms. Stefan smiled as if waiting for the opportune moment to pull her into his arms regardless of Mary's presence. She snuggled closer to the corner and laid her head against the glass window.

"Sulking?" Stefan asked in his silky deep voice.

Rosalind didn't answer.

"Ah, so you're ignoring me. Very mature, Rosalind, but why do I care if you wish to spend the entire journey cuddled into a corner when I've brought our picnic with us. I don't believe we had time to enjoy one on the day of your real birthday as promised. Though if memory serves, we did enjoy other activities."

At the mention of food her head snapped up involuntarily. She felt suddenly ravenous. Leave it to Stefan to hint towards any sort of inappropriate behavior within the same sentence.

They hadn't even had her birthday picnic and drat if she didn't feel her eyes well with tears that he would remember! But she didn't need to look as pleased as she felt, especially when her face felt so heated. For food was the last thing on her mind when that man's beautiful lips said the word *activities*.

"We wouldn't want the food to spoil," she said in a small voice.

"Ah, she speaks."

"Well?" Rosalind ignored his remark. "Where is our picnic?"

He flashed a brilliant grin. "Sweetheart, you must be so very hungry. Unfortunately, and I assure you it humbles me to no end to admit this to you, but that look in your eyes is for food and not my lessons." He sighed, and then moved his legs. On the floor next to his large outstretched feet lay a lumpy blanket. He pulled the blanket off revealing quite a nice little meal.

"Oh, my dear, oh dear, this simply will not do!" Mary put her knitting down and fanned in front of her face. "I cannot be in this carriage. Stop! Stop I say!"

"Is she having an apoplexy?" Stefan asked, then flinched when Mary's cane went flying wildly inside their tiny space.

"Oh, stop, stop, stop!" Mary yelled. If anything, the woman had just proved to everyone within a square mile that she had a healthy set of lungs at such an old age.

The carriage stopped, she hopped out, and Stefan watched as she climbed up top to where the footman was sitting. After bundling herself in a blanket she nodded her head and the carriage took off.

Rosalind sat motionless and angry. Mary and her reaction to any sort of food that carried even a hint of the color pink, was truly too much.

"What just happened?" Stefan had his hands in the air in total bewilderment.

"Well, to be truthful she despises anything resembling pink." Rosalind shrugged.

"It is beef. It's more red than anything," Stefan argued. "Blast if I knew pink to be such an intimidating color."

"Yes well, to her it has pink edges, so she had to leave." Rosalind rolled her eyes in exasperation.

"Right." Stefan still looked confused. "Will she be back?"

Rosalind contemplated lying but thought better of it because she was so blasted hungry. "No, I assume she'll stay next to the footman and Alfred until it gets too cold for her tender disposition."

"Tender disposition my—"

"—At any rate," Rosalind interrupted. "It was my birthday yesterday, and you did promise me a picnic. Are we to eat it or simply discuss it?"

"Have I told you how much I admire your moods? All twenty of them. And how you so effectively go from one to the other, quite exciting for a man. I'm never quite sure which woman I'll have the fortune to talk to. Most excitement I've had in months I assure you."

"The food?" Rosalind repeated.

"As you wish." Stefan pulled out a bottle of wine, rolls, meat pies, and some beef.

The smell of fresh food filled the entire carriage. Closing her eyes, Rosalind leaned back and inhaled the scent.

The noise of preparation stopped. She opened one eye and watched Stefan watch her and very slowly uncork the wine, all the while never taking his eyes off her throat. His unblinking stare could seduce a woman out of her good sense.

"Only barbarians stare with such hunger in their eyes," Rosalind stated as Stefan's eyes slowly closed halfway, becoming more hooded with desire by the second.

He shifted in his seat and looked quite uncomfortable with his legs stretching around the carriage. "Apologies, it seems age agrees with you. I found myself wondering how old you turned yesterday?"

Rosalind looked away and felt herself flush. "Old enough to be on the shelf, Your Grace."

"Deuced lucky shelf," he muttered pouring her a glass of wine and lifting her spirits at the exact same time.

Rosalind received the glass of wine and laughed. His large hands moved delicately over the foods as he chose her delicacies and then handed her the plate.

"Your food, my lady."

"You make a good servant, Stefan."

He threw his head back and laughed. "I'm good at everything. Including serving a deserving woman on her very important day, even if I'm a trifle late. Though to be fair, I had this brilliant plan on your actual birthday, so I believe credit and praise is still due." He winked.

"You know, my father once told me a woman's birthday is the most confusing day of her life."

Rosalind nibbled at her meat pie. "Why is that?"

"Well," Stefan helped himself to his own food, "it's the one time of year that reminds a woman that her youth is behind her, and more mature years are ahead of her. Women seem to speculate over years gone by with either regret or fondness. And swear to make the next year better than the last. If they do not meet their own expectations a birthday can be devastating. Yet another reminder that time is going by too fast."

"Then why is it also the happiest? That sounds dreadfully sad."

"Yes." Stefan sipped his wine. "It can also be a joy filled day."

Rosalind couldn't wait to hear what his definition of a woman's joy may be. No doubt he would say it had to do with a woman getting married or having a man to share her life with.

"It can be the happiest day of a woman's life because she has finally learned the one universal truth about herself."

Here it came.

"That with age, she becomes wise, self assured and confident. Consequently, the happiest women in the world are the ones that understand birthdays are a symbol of beauty. For there is nothing more attractive to a man than a woman who has truly lived. She who wears her age gracefully and with pride. Yes, birthdays for a woman are special. If anything, they announce to the world that you continue to grow more beautiful with time, like a rose coming into full bloom." Stefan leaned forward placing his large hand on Rosalind's leg. "And you, my dear, grow more beautiful each day I see you. I gather each minute you age represents another man's heart breaking with sorrow that you will never share your life or your bed alongside them."

Rosalind, quite literally had no idea what to say. In all her speeches about wooing, she had completely underestimated the man. His eyes crinkled into a smile and he went about his meal as if the sudden temperature in the carriage hadn't changed, as if she wasn't now positively charged with desire for him and confused as to where on earth he had come up with such beautiful words.

They ate their meal in silence and Rosalind found herself stealing glances in his direction constantly trying to find a chink in his armor. His arrogance it seemed was the only thing that still existed. She held onto that truth with a vice grip knowing if it was to shatter as well — she would have no reason not to allow herself to love him, and her heart simply could not take loving a man who did not love her back.

CHAPTER TEN

Love is a spirit all compact of fire.
~ Venus and Adonis 151 ~

INSERT MIND-NUMBING SILENCE here with a large dose of madness, Stefan thought for the tenth time as he watched his delightful companion once again pull into herself as if she were hiding something. Well, it was of no matter. They would arrive by nightfall and in the time leading up to it he would do everything in his power to persuade her to see things his way.

Stefan watched through hooded eyes as Rosalind continued to shift in her seat until, irritated, he reached across the carriage and laid a hand gently across her thigh. His only intention was to stop her from moving, lest he throw her out of the carriage to join her mad godmother, but as his hand rested across her dress, it was as if every nerve could feel the heat emitting from the woman.

"Be still," he croaked.

Rosalind eyed him pensively before making a grand gesture of folding her hands in her lap and sighing.

"Shall I bribe you with sweets, my lady?" His hand was still frozen on her person; it would take a lot more than a pensive look from the lady to get him to remove any part of his body from hers, regardless of propriety.

Rosalind licked her lips, still not meeting his gaze. "Resorting to bribery? Interesting. It must be so terribly uncomfortable for you to sit in silence, Your Grace."

"The silence, it seems, is not one of my current grievances," he glanced down at his hand and then dipped his gaze to her parted lips.

"Sweets, you say?" She pushed his hand away and straightened her skirts.

"Ah, it seems I need to resort to many things in order to gain your approval and the pleasure of your conversation. Yes, fairy cakes to be exact. It is, after all your birthday."

Rosalind didn't respond. Sighing, he rummaged through the picnic basket and withdrew two wrapped fairy cakes. Slowly, he unfolded one cake and held out his hand.

She looked doubtful and mistrusting as her hand reached across the small carriage and quickly swiped the fairy cake away from his clutches. Wise decision on her part, considering he used the opportunity to grab her other wrist and pull her into his lap. Rosalind wasn't quick enough for his advance; nay his attack, and he relished the feeling of her bottom moving against him while at the same time hating himself for enjoying her torture. Well it wasn't as if he was getting any release from her anytime soon, so truthfully they were torturing each other.

Fighting him, she finally relented fairy cake in hand, but now his prisoner. He smiled at his fortune and brilliance as her chest heaved up and down in frustration. Caught like a rat with its cheese.

"That was not fair."

Stefan continued grinning. "Didn't you know Rosalind?

Men, rarely play fair, or was it women? I get confused, but I do recall you repeating something similar to your good friend, Lord Rawlings."

Her eyes narrowed.

"It seems, your desire for a fairy cake trumped your logic and good thinking, for it was the bait in which I used to secure you, therefore making it possible to woo you the rest of the way to London." Which meant he had still but six hours to convince her to be his.

"Your Grace, if trapping a woman through sweets is another one of your ways of seduction, you are without a doubt the worst seducer to grace the country."

"Says the trapped little bird."

She squirmed under his brace, her bottom moving to and fro. His smile grew larger as blood roared through his veins. "My, my, how you play so deliciously into my hand."

"What do you want?" She relented her squirming and looked sadly down at the fairy cake.

"I want to feed you your birthday cake." He shrugged simply as if it was the most natural thing to do with a woman in a carriage.

"And if I allow it?"

"Then my wooing for the day is finished. I only ask that you endure as best you can."

"Endure..." She looked down at the fairy cake in hand. "And you promise to stop trying to seduce and woo me. And no more lessons?"

"For the remainder of the day, yes."

"I agree."

"I'm sorry it appears with age my hearing as declined. What did you say, my dear?"

A muscle twitched in her cheek as she answered through clenched teeth, "Do not push it, Your Grace. I said I agree and I mean it."

"Wonderful," he released her arms and very carefully lifted her from his lap to the seat next to him. "Now, let's have the fairy cake, and I'll show you the proper way to eat such a delicacy in celebration of one's birthday."

Her shoulders slumped as she guilty handed over the fairy cake.

"Now," he grinned and unfolded the napkin holding the cake on his lap. "The best way to enjoy cake on ones birthday is blindfolded." Her indignant huff nearly did him in as he reached into the basket and pulled out a small napkin and motioned for her to turn so he could fasten it around her head. "Can you see anything?"

"No, but I gather that's the idea." She turned to face him and he found the idea that she couldn't see him sinfully erotic as his eyes boldly took in her plump bottom lip. Perhaps just a nibble...

"Perfect." He cleared his throat. "Now, open your mouth."

First, she nibbled her lips then apparently the idea of having a fairy cake won out, like a little bird ready to be fed, she opened her bow lips. He found he couldn't merely hand over the food and be done with this little experiment to get her to trust him. So, instead he dipped his finger in frosting and swiped it across her bottom lip.

Her pink tongue emerged and licked her bottom lip and he found himself once again entranced by her motions. Rosalind relaxed, just slightly, and Stefan found himself needing to see her eyes as she enjoyed the fairy cake. He pulled off the blindfold and stared in awe as her eyelashes blinked slowly at him then closed in ecstasy, giving Stefan the jealous feeling that he was missing out on the exchange between the participant and the object — frosting.

Suddenly, the carriage came to a halt. Stefan bellowed a curse as the door swung open. "I just cannot take the cold any longer, Your Grace. To think that you allowed me to even step outside the carriage is quite beyond me. Really you should have more manners. Oh, fairy cakes! Don't mind if I do!" Mary swiped the cake out of his grasp and comfortably positioned herself on the other side of the carriage.

Dumbstruck, Stefan didn't know if it was at all proper to say out loud the obscenities he was thinking in his head considering there was a lady present. Mary didn't count.

Rosalind smirked at him and he found himself helpless as to how to continue on without, one getting caned, and two aroused quite awkwardly as the godmother held a blunt object within her grasp.

The footman was still standing outside the door, mouth ajar, the poor bloke was probably already thinking of where to seek other employment after allowing a passenger in the duke's carriage to put a stop to their journey.

Stefan nodded his head towards the pale man and told him to get on with it. The man scrambled to shut the door and soon they were off.

"I gather you're over your aversion to our picnic?" Stefan dusted his hands of the stolen fairy cake.

"Well, if you wouldn't have been so belligerent with your waving of that horrid-looking meat, I wouldn't have had to step outside of the carriage, Your Grace."

"Are you scolding me?" He felt his chest rise as his fingers clenched into the seat.

"Nonsense," Rosalind piped up, gently touching the top of his clenched hand. "Mary was merely pointing out that we were insensitive to her…"

"Delicacies." Stefan finished through clenched teeth.

Rosalind turned giving him a blinding smile. "Precisely."

Well, he couldn't exactly argue with the girl considering his mouth had suddenly gone dry, and she hadn't let go of his hand. The warmth from her skin seeped through her kid gloves and Stefan silently wondered if it was possible for a man to go insane from one touch.

"We should be in London within the next few hours," he said.

Rosalind winked while Mary continued to argue about the cold, and Stefan couldn't help himself from turning over his hand and grasping Rosalind's delicate fingers. He also couldn't help but smile triumphantly as her hand grasped his back, hidden beneath her skirts it seemed all was well within the world. Propriety be damned.

He was holding her hand.

And Stefan had trouble remembering a hand that had ever fit so beautifully within his.

Thump! Stefan jolted awake. He must have fallen asleep near the end of the trip. The carriage was stopped, why was it stopped?

Rosalind awoke from her slumber as did Mary and unfortunately her cane got a good waving about before she managed to calm herself enough to know the carriage was not in fact tipped on its side.

He'd be lucky to survive that cane. In fact, he made a mental note to hide it first thing in London.

"I'll just be a minute." Stefan rapped on the door. The footman opened it to let him out. "What seems to be the problem?"

"Sorry, Your Grace. The horse, it seems to have thrown a shoe."

"Where are we?" he asked ignoring the horrid news.

"Just over yonder hill is the Knights Inn, Your Grace. If we stay there for a few hours, I'm sure we can fix the problem."

The sun was beginning to set. It was a stretch to have made the trip in one day as it was. And he wasn't exactly thrilled that they would have to travel through the night in order to make it to London.

"We shall stay at the Inn over night."

"But—" the footman's nostrils flared.

"Well what is it?" Stefan was irritated and tired of sitting next to Rosalind for so long.

"Well, Your Grace. It's just that, well…"

Alfred hopped down from his seat, "Your Grace, forgive me but it wouldn't be proper to spend the night alone unchaperoned."

"I'm sure Mary is a proper chaperone. She has a blasted cane Alfred, and she glares at me as if she intends to make any excuse to use it. Lady Rosalind's virtue will be intact, I assure you. My sanity however, is still in question."

"Very good, sir." Alfred bowed and motioned for the groom to bring the horse. Samson neighed at Stefan, though he could have sworn it was mockery the way it sounded coming from his beloved horse. Another night, alone, with this woman and he was going to go mad. Truly, his curse must be Rosalind, for he hadn't slept a wink since laying eyes on her.

"Let us be off, Samson." He pulled at the reigns and knocked on the carriage door. "Ladies, it seems we are to be taking a short respite for the night. Rosalind, if you would be so kind as to accompany me on Samson, we'll just be off to the nearest Inn over the hill."

"And what of Mary?" she asked stepping down.

"She shall stay with Alfred, he will be sure to take great care of her."

Mary blushed like a schoolgirl. Bewildered, Stefan looked at his valet only to see him with a similar rosy hue.

"Well?" Rosalind said standing in front of him.

Stefan shook his head. "Right, off we go." He mounted

Samson and held his arm to Rosalind. With little effort, she was on the horse behind him. And dash it all if Samson didn't seem to be proud as he neighed, pranced, and snorted.

"Show off," Stefan muttered. Samson neighed and lifted his head. Stefan rolled his eyes in disgust, pleading to the heavens yet again for a horse that wouldn't take attention away from him.

"He's really such a lovely horse." Rosalind said with a throaty laugh.

"Yes, my thoughts exactly." Stefan clenched his teeth and pulled tight on the reigns. Shown up by his horse... again.

The smell of horse mixed with sweat and leather pounded into Rosalind's senses. The last thing she needed was to be trapped in a small inn with a man of Stefan's nature.

She was beyond being worried or irritated or perhaps even frightened at the prospect. Fear and excitement twisted inside her gut until she thought she would surely expire from the turmoil of her circumstances. Why couldn't they merely change horses and ride through the night? Surely it wouldn't take that long to reach London!

"Sorry, Rose. It seems that we were already behind schedule as it was. We would have needed to stop regardless. Naturally, I blame Mary." Stefan muttered as they reached the top of the hill and were able to see the inn. She desperately wanted to be back at the carriage. At least then her body wouldn't be awkwardly pressed against his. Sitting side-saddle behind him made it difficult to concentrate on anything but the way her arms fit around his waist, or the hard planes of his muscles as they clenched and twitched beneath hers. Would it be so terrible to lay her head down on him?

"Rose?" he prompted.

"Really, it's not trouble at all!" Rosalind feigned any sort of confidence she could muster up. "Truly, we shall arrive in the afternoon."

Stefan shrugged and started to whistle. It appeared his only aim when he could sense her frustration was to drive her mad with that ridiculous tune! And why the devil did he constantly whistle the same thing? Was his creativity in the same category as his romance?

Not that his romance was at all lacking. Quite the opposite in fact, which was why in her desperation and worrisome thoughts she found herself nearly bruising her lip as she bit down in concentration.

Stefan hopped off the horse and held his hand to her. With reluctance, she conceded and with a swift prayer slid off of Samson straight into the barbarian's arms.

Magic. It had always been as such when his firm body came into contact with hers. There was no release. As if sensing her need, her desire — her want. His muscled arms bracketed around her.

"In the mood for more lessons, sweetheart?"

Breath coming out in short gasps, Rosalind could only shake her head and close her eyes as his forehead leaned against hers.

"Why do you fight it so?" Stefan whispered.

"What woman would not fight what she does not have any semblance of control over?"

He smirked. "What woman would desire to control something so passionate?"

His arms continued to encircle her as he lifted his head and laid a soft warm kiss on the curve of her neck. The faint brush of his hair tickled down her collarbone as she memorized the way his lips felt against her skin.

"Don't fight me, love. I only want—"

"Your Grace, so sorry for interrupting, but you may want

to acquire rooms. It seems to be quite busy!" the footman said apologetically as he turned his cherry red face away from the couple and cleared his throat.

Warmth immediately left Rosalind as Stefan pulled away and straightened his jacket. "Of course. Shall we, my Rose?"

Rosalind gave a short awkward nod and took his arm.

CHAPTER ELEVEN

We are such stuff
As dreams are made on, And our little life
Is rounded with a sleep.
~ The Tempest ~

STEFAN SCANNED THE CROWDS of people as they neared the inn. It would be a miracle for them to find a room, let alone two. Knowing he was without any solid option other than claiming Rosalind as a wife, he approached the innkeeper and prepared for battle, for the woman next to him would rather be trampled by Samson then announce to the world that they were married.

"My good man, my wife and I are in need of two of your best rooms."

Rosalind began choking. Stefan used the opportunity to pull her closer into his frame. All the while trying desperately not to grin as she stiffened beneath his hold.

"Wedding night. She's a tad frightened." He gave a little wink to the innkeeper, who abruptly started laughing as if they were sharing a small joke at Rosalind's expense.

Then the woman drove her heel into his boot sending a yelp of pain out of Stefan's mouth before he could stop it.

Rosalind smirked. "Sorry sir, it seems my husband is nursing some fears of his own as well. Aren't you husband?" She turned to look at the innkeeper. "Seems tonight will be a night of many firsts. Can you imagine? A duke as innocent as this one!" Rosalind sent an elbow sailing into Stefan's stomach. "Now, about those rooms."

The innkeeper smiled revealing two rotting teeth. "Yes, well you see, we only have."

"One room?" Rosalind guessed.

Stefan winced. Leave it to Rosalind to make an even bigger spectacle; more than likely she would start shouting at any minute.

"Yes, my lady, or Your Grace?" He said it as a question, apparently still not sure with whom he was conversing.

"The Duchess of Montmouth, but we need to keep it a secret. You see I ran away to escape my evil mother only to be rescued by this brute here and his glorious horse—"

"—here we go." Stefan muttered a curse and shook his head.

"His horse is lovely, by the way." Rosalind patted the innkeeper's hand. He leaned forward with obvious rapture at Rosalind's treatment of him. "Where was I? Oh yes, the rescue! So, as I was saying. The duke here came searching for me as a man would his long lost princess and now we are returning to claim what is rightfully ours!"

The innkeeper sighed. "That's a lovely story, Your Grace."

"Indeed," Stefan grumbled.

"And can you imagine that this one here didn't even offer me a proper proposal?" Her finger pointed directly into Stefan's face making him sweat profusely under his tight fitting jacket. Devil take it, where was the air in that tiny hole?

"No proposal, Miss?" A woman came up behind the innkeeper and shook her head. "What type of man doesn't propose to the woman he rescues?"

Somehow, Rosalind managed watery eyes as she shook her head in feigned sadness. "He merely said we must marry at once!"

Both gasped.

"And you haven't heard the worst of it."

Stefan tugged on Rosalind's arm. "I'm sure they don't need to hear—"

"He took advantage of me being without a chaperone, and he still hasn't wooed me!"

"Woo?" the innkeeper said as the woman continued to shake her head.

"Yes, woo." Rosalind confirmed.

The innkeeper looked to Stefan. "Did you try flowers?"

"Or sonnets?" The woman chimed in clapping her hands.

Expletives poured out of Stefan's mouth before he was able to say anything remotely appropriate. Unfortunately, his goal had not in fact been to appall everyone, including himself, though he succeeded admirably if the shocked expressions on everyone's faces were any indication. Had he lost all control over himself? His horse would be doing a better job than he at this moment! Wincing, he pinched the bridge of his nose and looked away.

"Your Grace." The lady shook her head somberly at Rosalind as if she felt sorry for the obvious hardship she was undertaking in accepting Stefan's proposal of marriage. "I will prepare the best of rooms for you and your brute of a husband. Now, why don't you go over and have yourself a nice cup of tea while my husband here gives yours some pointers. Surely he needs them! To think a virgin man who demands women to marry him without any sort of romance!

Well, I'm troubled by it!"

"Virgin!" Stefan roared.

"Shhh…" the lady hushed him. "All will be well. Your fear will hold you back no longer, Your Grace."

Stefan had several things at the tip of his tongue that he wanted to say, none of them appropriate. "My wife, it seems has been misleading. I'm not afraid." He choked somehow on his tongue, as it became like sand in his mouth. Why was he so blasted nervous?

"Off you go!" the woman called to Rosalind. The girl smiled triumphantly as she strutted over to a small table.

"Conniving, impetuous, manipulative—"

"Your Grace?" The innkeeper cleared his throat. "Now, I'll have the room ready in a small bit. We need to do some—" *Cough* "—rearranging of our guests, so if you'd like a tankard of ale or whiskey while you wait, I can easily…" He cleared his throat again. "That is to say, I can go over a few specifics for such a night, if you—"

"I am not virgin!" Stefan shouted, drawing the attention of every eye in the room and more than likely every ear on the continent. Men and women everywhere burst out laughing.

He was going to kill her.

Slowly.

And then pleasure her until she couldn't take it.

And promptly leave her — alone, cold and in the bed without any way to rid herself of the heightened lovemaking and the emotions that went with it.

"You're smiling, Your Grace. I take it your fear has lessened." The innkeeper lifted an eyebrow.

"Immensely, thank you for your… talk." He shook the man's hand and went to sit by the little chit who thought making a laughingstock out of him would keep his more carnal instincts at bay.

She was in for a rude awakening.

Or possibly just an awakening like none other, and he couldn't wait to be the one man to bring her to her knees.

His happiness at pleasuring her trumped his desire to strangle her as he made his way to where the manipulative little thing sat.

"Oh, the virgin approaches!" Rosalind lifted her cup of tea with a snicker.

Stefan opened his mouth to give her a good set down, but she interrupted.

"I find your need to control everything extremely aggravating."

Stefan slammed his ale on the counter. "Well, I find your need to embarrass a man in front of a large group of people infuriating!"

"It helped!"

"Oh, good. The insane woman thinks it helped! Well, perfect! And just how did you announcing that little tidbit to the entirety of the inn help, sweetheart?"

"You'll see." She winked.

Stefan continued to glare at Rosalind as her dainty lips parted every so often in order to drink her tea. Scowling, he crossed his arms across his chest and tried not to think about that delectable mouth of hers. The same mouth that had the power to bring him to his knees or make him want to throttle her with one breath.

Just how long did it take to ready such a room, anyway? Just as Stefan was contemplating making a move to ask the innkeeper, Rosalind's eyes locked onto something behind him.

He turned around.

"Your Grace?" The innkeeper's wife approached. "Your rooms are ready if you'll just follow me." A slight blush stained her cheeks as she led them up the stairs and down the hall to the farthest door at the end.

"'Tis our best room. Though we've only a small inn, we

wanted to give you as much privacy as you needed." The blush deepened.

Stefan clenched his teeth and sent a seething glare to Rosalind, who merely gave him that confident shrug he found so blasted irritating.

"We are so very honored you have chosen to stay with us tonight." She unlocked the door and handed Stefan the key before rushing out of sight.

"Well…" Stefan looked to Rosalind. "May as well make the lie believable."

And with that he pulled Rosalind into his arms and carried her across the threshold, fighting with everything in him not to actually blush at the cheer that came from below the stairs.

With a grunt, he pushed the door open. And promptly dropped the very woman he was carrying onto the cold hard ground.

Rosalind squeaked as she hit the floor with a thud. Stefan smirked and reached to pull her to her feet, but she slapped him away with dainty hands.

"Mind allowing me the courtesy of knowing why in heaven's name you would drop me?" She seethed.

Unfortunately, Rosalind's cheeks were rosy and vibrant. Pieces of hair had all but fallen out of her coiffure and rested very slightly against her soft face. In that instant, Stefan felt himself blush. Actually experienced the feeling of all the blood rushing to his face — his need, his desire, and actual embarrassment over the shameful things he was going to do to her came barreling forward into his consciousness as he looked at the beautiful woman in front of him, and the breath-taking room they had been given.

A bath was drawn, the smell of rose water fresh in the air. A small dinner and bottle of wine sat in the corner and in all her haste the innkeeper's wife was still able to scatter about tiny little candles everywhere, which he knew would be expensive for such a small inn. It seemed to have remnants of a romantic night full of pleasure and fantasy everywhere. The darkness of the room draped in candlelight sent chills through his body. Selfishly he wanted it to be real. All of it... and he wondered if he had already ruined everything by his careless proposals.

He truly expected Samson to burst his head through the windows covered in roses. A more magical room he had never before seen.

At least that was what he thought, until his eyes took their fill of Rosalind as she twirled around the enchanted room and laughed.

In his head, it happened like a slow aching dream. Vibrant red hair danced around her shoulders, green eyes closed in rapture. Long black eyelashes fanned against her high cheekbones, and her sultry laugh rang through the room. Absorbed, he could only continue to watch and curse himself for truly feeling like a virgin.

Biting back an oath, Stefan swallowed the lump of emotion in his throat. Finally, she stopped her twirling and looked at him.

He desperately wished she would have continued, for then he wouldn't have to see the clarity of her eyes, the bewitching beauty of her face, nor the cursed lift of her chin as she awaited his apology.

"Sorry, I was wrong. Did you want to bathe first?" The words were rushed and foreign as they flowed from his lips. Stefan's feet took him opposite Rosalind in the room. He needed to stay away from the warmth of her body. He hadn't meant for the words to tumble out of his mouth as fast as they did, and hoped she would be grateful that he at least admitted his wrong.

"I'm sorry, what was that?" Rosalind asked.

"An apology."

"Oh. The clarification is much appreciated; I wasn't able to hear the full apology considering you weren't actually looking in my direction. Weren't you scolding me of that very thing the day before last?"

Must women remember everything? "I will admit to doing so, yes. And…" he exhaled as he turned to look at her. "I apologize, for my harshness earlier, and for my anger." *As well as threatening to pleasure you then promptly leave.*

"Accepted." White teeth bit across her bottom lip as she put her hands on her hips in thought. "I believe I'll bathe first, since the spoils of war are mine, Your Grace."

Brilliant. She was the type to rub in defeat. How fortunate for him. "I'll just be downstairs then." Turning in every direction but the door he needed to exit, Stefan was finally able to make his escape, though the echo of Rosalind's mocking laughter from within the room was enough to cause him the desire to barge in on her bath. After all, she was to be his wife in mere days, that is, if he could get his proposals correct. And learn how to romance better than his horse.

Apparently the cards were stacked quite heavily against him. With a grunt, he kicked the side of the wall with his polished boot. It did wonders for his outlook on life. If only he could join Mary and Alfred in the stables, perhaps then his lust would cool. Yes, a toss in the hay that was exactly what he needed. Except that, when his brain thought of tossing and hay together, it conjured up images of Rosalind in the hay. Grunting, he kicked the wall again as he made his way back down for a tankard of ale. The poorly lit establishment at least offered ale that didn't taste sour. He managed a small smile as he downed his first tankard and looked around at the rest of the patrons. Now if he could just get his lust for the woman out of his mind so he could have a peaceful night's sleep without waking up with aching need.

Perhaps he would have two tankards.

CHAPTER TWELVE

I know a lady in Venice who would have walked barefoot
To Palestine for a taste of his nether lip.
~ Othello — William Shakespeare ~

ROSALIND SLIPPED OUT OF her traveling dress with a moan. Unfortunately the moan made her think of Stefan, which was entirely improper, not that she could help it. The man was a virile god compared to those she was used to associating with. It was why, in her mind, she needed to be his intellectual equal on all planes, for when he smiled, or even touched her. All bets were off.

With a little twisting she was able to rid herself of her corset, chemise, and stockings. The hot water looked divine and inviting. With glee she lifted her leg into the water. Rosalind closed her eyes and allowed herself to relax into the hot bath. After a while, she thought it would be best to actually wash so that Stefan could return. Yawning, she reached for the soap.

A fierce pounding at the door caused her to jump with

fright. "Open up, Rosalind. I've changed my mind." It could hardly be considered a knock for the brute was nearly taking the door down with all the force he was using. What the devil did that savage want!

"No!" she yelled, unladylike and loud enough to give him the idea that he was not welcome during her peaceful bath time.

"Yes!" Stefan roared. "We are to be husband and wife, Rosalind, and I will not stand out here like some boy wet behind the ears because I cannot at least sit in the room with a woman I'm attracted to while she bathes."

"The self control of a saint, I'm sure!" Rosalind mocked.

"You have my word, I'll turn around, I just cannot be down with the rest of the patrons any longer."

"And why is that, Your Grace?"

A long silence ensued. "They keep referring to… it."

Rosalind grabbed the long dressing robe left by the innkeeper's wife and wrapped it around her body. "Your Grace, I believe you're going to need to be more specific as to what it is."

"Allow me entrance, and I will."

"This door opens when you tell me."

"Virginity," he mumbled.

Rosalind covered her mouth in laughter. "Are they teasing you, Your Grace?"

Another long drawn out silence. "Yes."

"Very well, but you must close your eyes; otherwise, I'll bring Mary in here with her cane. No telling what she may do if she sees me in my current state of undress with you present."

"Agreed." Stefan said.

Reaching for the door, Rosalind allowed herself one more burst of laughter before she pulled it open revealing a slightly red and if appearance was any indicator, possibly foxed

Stefan.

"How much ale have you consumed?" she asked.

Stefan pushed past her, not even glancing at her robe. "Not enough, Rose. Not enough." He cursed under his breath as he walked to the window then back again to the door, slamming it closed. As his hand rested across the wood, he stood, nay swayed in front of her, then turned on his heel and went to the bed and closed his eyes. "You may proceed."

Why did she get the feeling that she was a courtesan? "Close your eyes, Your Grace."

"I assure you, I have no desire to be caned, Rosalind. Take your bath, and be quick about it, my muscles ache and my pride is non-existent. I want nothing more than to drown myself in your bath water in hopes of erasing my memory of the Innkeeper showing me the proper way to kiss a lady."

The man was making it torture not to burst out laughing. Putting her hand over her mouth, Rosalind waited a minute before answering. Saints alive! The last person on God's green earth that needed to learn how to properly kiss a woman was Stefan. If anything he was too skilled for words. The man should be teaching others how to kiss and properly make a lady a pile of wantonness. After a few minutes, she felt she was able to answer without giving him clue to her amusement. "I'm sure that was very hard on you, Stefan."

"Yes, well. Difficult and hard circumstances have been an everyday occurrence in your presence. I may just cane myself by the end of our little trip. Perhaps your godmother will do me the courtesy."

"And have Mary miss out?" Rosalind laughed. "I doubt she would be pleased." She stepped around the screen and threw off the robe. Goosebumps rose across her flesh as she took a step into the tub and slowly sank down into the warmth.

"Ahhh." She moaned aloud, completely lost in ecstasy.

"Rosalind," Stefan said hoarsely.

"Hmm?"

"If you could possibly keep yourself from moaning in ecstasy, I would be much obliged. I find my ears quite sensitive to feminine noises and my body extremely willing to join you. If you care for your own virginity, it would be best to be silent."

"Understood," she croaked, sinking lower into the bath and hoping for it to swallow her whole.

Rosalind made quick work of her bath and was attaching the dressing gown just as Stefan asked if she was finished. With a sigh she answered yes and walked to the fireplace to allow her hair to dry in the warm heat.

She felt Stefan approach and looked up at his menacing form. Broad arms were crossed against his chest. Dark eyes darted around the room to everything but her. "I won't have you watching me."

"Your Grace, the last thing my virgin mind wants is to see a savage without his clothes. Now hurry with your bath so we can enjoy the meal before it gets cold."

He grunted, and turned towards the where the bath was laid out. Rosalind shook her head in front of the fire and leaned back on the floor to gain closer access to the fiery flames.

With a splash, she assumed Stefan had indeed found out a way to gain access into the bath without tripping in his semi-foxed state. A musical whistle invaded her thoughts. Always that whistle, always that tune.

"What is the song you whistle so often?" she asked.

The whistling stopped. "It's called The Beast. Actually one of the earlier works of Dominique Makyslov, the man who happens to have your beloved title and lands."

"It's sad."

Stefan was silent for a while. "But the notes are fast paced are they not?"

"It's a sad song masquerading as a happy song," Rosalind said.

"That, it is. Very few actually understand the emotions of music, Rose."

"Very few people actually listen, Your Grace."

She closed her eyes again as he started the song anew, lost in the passion of a whistle was quite odd for her, it begged the question if Stefan was a musically gifted man who could also sing.

The fire continued to heat her skin, but suddenly it became much too hot. Curious, Rosalind opened her eyes to see the edges of her robe catching fire. With a scream she jumped up onto her feet.

"What, what is it!" Stefan was suddenly at her side his body a blur as he hit the flames with his bare feet before turning to her and examining her face. "Are you hurt? Did you get burned?"

"No, I'm not — Oh my—"

Stefan gave her a peculiar look and then glanced at himself. All of himself. For the man was standing in front of her sans any clothing covering his gloriously sculpted body.

"I—I—uh..." Rosalind began to speak but found no words. Nothing, to describe the longing she felt all over her body. The fascination she found in gazing upon his. Hard muscled plans over his stomach, broad shoulders fit for a king. And skin so smooth she wanted to reach out and touch it.

Unfortunately, that was exactly what she did, and immediately regretted it as fire seemed to burst into Stefan's eyes.

"Don't," he said grabbing her hand forcefully within his. The grip he had on her was strong.

Her hand shook under the pressure of his. Eyes black with desire he pulled her flush against all of him. "I mean to propose to you, to be a romantic. Not to take you and force a marriage upon you in that way."

Rosalind could only nod and watch as his eyes took their fill of her lips. With a curse, he crushed his lips against hers, savagely, passionately pulling more and more of her until she thought she would die. Stefan's body was still wet from the bath, warm water only seemed to ignite her skin as it soaked through her robe. His arms braced tightly around her, one hand stroked her neck then dove lower. Her robe was haphazardly thrown on and she hadn't worn a chemise underneath. Now she was grateful for it as Stefan's hand easily plunged into the opening, pulling it half off in the process. His mouth pressed against hers harder as he sucked and nipped, and then abruptly as it started, he ended the kiss.

"No!" He released her quickly and stomped back to the bath spilling water everywhere as he jumped in and giving her quite a glorious view of his backside as he did so.

"Leave." Voice shaking he closed his eyes and sank back against the tub. "Rose, please, just… go downstairs and ask the innkeeper's wife for some more wine. Can you do that?"

Rosalind couldn't answer, and it wasn't as if she was wearing a traveling dress. "I'm not dressed to—"

"—then turn around and cease from making any sort of feminine noise or sigh or moan. In fact, if you could suddenly pick up the art of not breathing for a few moments, I would be much obliged."

"You want me to stop breathing?"

"Just… be still," he whispered.

Rosalind quickly sat in the chair and closed her eyes. Truly, she did try to focus on keeping her breathing even but she found the more she tried the harder it became. And images of Stefan's magnificent body seemed imprinted into her mind so vividly that she found her breathing picked up!

His bath continued, and she only knew this because she

heard splashing and after several minutes, a different tune.

Stefan cursed in French, German, and his very own made up language — all in his head of course for he didn't want to alarm Rosalind. No, the poor girl was probably at this moment contemplating ways to wear all her clothing in hopes to battle untoward advances from him.

What the devil did she think he would do? He was a man! When a woman screams, a man is there to protect! And Rosalind, curse the woman. She was everything to him. Protecting her was like breathing, so when he heard her scream a panic like none other enveloped him. Obviously without thinking, he ran to her aid. Only to find, too late, that he was grossly unprepared for a lust filled battle as her eyes boldly scanned his naked body.

Never had he felt a more screaming desire to take a woman to bed. To fully consume a woman. His hands ached to reach out and touch her. His body pounded with the desire. As the blood roared through his ears, as the lust blinded his sound mind making everything he was about to do justifiable. He looked into her eyes and paused.

Trust.

He had finally gained it. And was in no position to lose it. The kiss was a gut instinct, a mistake. A way to capture a taste of what he had become so addicted to over the past few days. Instead, it nearly ruined everything, and he wasn't at all sure how to go about the night. Perhaps pretend that he wasn't fearful of ravishing her? His semi-foxed state did nothing to help circumstances.

With a sigh, he finished his bath and donned his breeches and shirtsleeves, in hopes to cover himself up more than before. Stefan took a seat next to the small table with the food.

"You may open your eyes now, Rose."

She opened her eyes and tentatively rose from the chair and sat opposite him.

"May I be bold, Your Grace?" Rosalind's eyes were downcast as if she was thinking very carefully on something.

"Always," Stefan grinned trying to lighten the passion-filled mood.

"I find a man beautiful. I find you beautiful. And I cannot imagine my eyes ever seeing something that is your equal."

Stunned into silence, Stefan's mouth could only drop open as Rosalind blushed profusely and poured them wine.

He reached out and touched her shaking hand. "Perhaps no equal, but a beauty far surpasses my own. You need not but look in the mirror my Rose, to see my meaning."

They ate and drank in silence. Rosalind continued to look down. After the meal was finished she finally raised her eyes to meet his.

It was akin to getting punched in the stomach. He had to make this angel, this beautifully strong woman, his.

"Your song." She tilted her head. "It changed tunes."

"Ah, so you noticed." Amused, he leaned back against the chair and crossed his arms. "Another one of Dominique's beautiful piano fortes. Can you guess what it is about?"

"Death?" Rosalind joked.

Stefan scowled. "Try again."

"Horses?"

"Wrong, and I don't believe any songs have been written about Samson yet, but I wouldn't completely cross that probability from happening."

"Lust?" she squeaked.

"Close…" He leaned forward. "It's about desire."

"Oh."

"Yes." Stefan laughed. "Oh." He held out his hand to her. "Tell me, Rose. What do you know of desire?"

Her eyes darted to his outstretched hand and back to his face. "Women do not desire, or at least we are told not to."

"It will be a sad day for everyone if women listened to society's restrictions. Don't you think? Did you know that when I touch you, you blush? For such a strong independent woman, it pleases me immensely to see a chink in your confident attitude."

"Have you ever thought the blush was because you were making untoward advances, Your Grace? Perhaps, I do not appreciate your touch."

"Really?" Rising from his chair, Stefan walked over to Rosalind and knelt in front of her. "Does my touch then, cause a wanton response within you, my lady?"

"Immensely," she said breathless.

"Does my presence make you uncomfortable?"

"Always."

"Does my kiss cause you to weep with pain?"

"Daily."

"Then, sweetheart, you have experienced desire." Bestowing a kiss upon her hand, he winked, and returned to his chair. "Tell me of your mother." He needed to change the subject, lest she became filled with panic and decide to sleep with Samson. God forbid she sleep with horse before master.

The thought alone made him outwardly shudder.

"She isn't that evil," Rosalind said.

"Sorry, I was wool-gathering. Now, about your mother. Has she treated you fairly since your father's death?"

Rosalind looked down, her eyelashes casting a shadow across her cheeks. "If sending me away to die is any indication, than no, she has not treated me fairly."

"Tell me Rose, what kind of mother sends her daughter away to die?"

Rosalind shrugged. "One full of fear. I imagine she thought to stow me away, just like the curse. She blames us for my father's death. I believe it was too painful to watch me, and the sleeping spells don't help matters."

"Ah, yes, you're swooning spells."

"Fainting spells," she corrected.

"Yes, well I'd like to believe they are swooning spells, and that I'm solely responsible for their cause, if that isn't too hard for you to understand. Allow me this boon. After all, my pride has taken an enormous hit after this night."

Rosalind laughed. "Fine, my swooning spells are brought on by the great Duke of Montmouth."

"Much obliged."

"I haven't had them since returning to the country estate, I wonder why?"

Stefan shrugged. "Perhaps the great Duke of Montmouth is the cause and the cure."

"Your Grace!" Rosalind gasped with a smile.

"What? What is it?" Stefan looked around for a tiny rodent, or any sort of indicator for why Rosalind's face was so lit up.

"I believe you've recovered it!"

"Truly?" His chest pumped up involuntarily as she praised him.

"Why, yes! It seems your pride wasn't lost after all."

Blast! And why the devil did he feel his face heating? "Yes well, I just needed a little push in order to obtain that sense of male pride again. Many thanks."

She smirked. "Now that you know my sordid tale and reasons for why I despise having to return, allow me one question."

Heaven help him, he'd give her as many as she wanted. Never had he enjoyed a woman's company as much as he enjoyed hers. "Anything."

"Why did you go to India?"

The familiar pang of unrequited love didn't surface as he

thought it would with such a question. Instead, relief that he was no longer the green boy he once was. The infatuation with Elaina had been exactly that, an infatuation. And one he was pleased to be over with. How could a woman such as Elaina even hope to compete when Rosalind was alive and breathing?

"I believe—" He twisted uncomfortably in his chair. "—that tale, like so many others, begins with a young man's passion and a woman's rejection."

"I do love stories." Rosalind's excitement caught him off guard, and he found himself leaning forward to tell her the story.

"I was in love with her. I believed myself to be in love with her, but she was not for me. I left the country to escape living in hell. My father helped make arrangements and nobody was the wiser, except him. It was the coward's way out, but at the time I saw no other option other than living in extreme agony."

Rosalind squinted. "Leaving the country was a little extreme, was it not?"

"Love is extreme, my Rose. It causes even the sanest of the human population to wish for death. It is the stuff of poetry, war, death, and duels. Nothing is too extreme for love."

The fire spat, jolting Stefan out of his speech. Rosalind was affected by talk of love. Like any young woman, he noticed the soft sigh that escaped her billowy lips at his speech. Why then, was he so horrible at proposals? Truly, he wanted to know. For when he was in normal conversation with her, he felt romantic enough to quote Byron. When it came to asking her the one question he needed to ask, he sounded the greatest fool.

"The night gets late." His husky voice betrayed his thoughts.

"It is." Rosalind bit her lip and shot to her feet. "I'll just take the floor."

Stefan laughed. "Rosalind, the day you sleep on the floor is the day I'm dead and unable to argue with you about such ridiculous notions. You take the bed. A woman should never sleep on hard surfaces or in the dirt. I'm appalled you would suggest it."

Rosalind covered her yawn as her eyes smiled. Heaven help him, she was stunning, even when she was beyond exhaustion.

"Off you go." He motioned for her to move to the bed. "I'll turn my back while you crawl beneath the blankets.

He turned around and nearly died with unquenched desire as he heard the rustling of the blankets and squeak of the bed.

"You may turn around now, Stefan."

Blankets covered her from chin to toe. Pity, for he would have liked to see a bit more considering she'd already seen all of him.

With a deep sigh, he ran one hand through his thick hair and approached the bed. "Sleep well, my beauty, my little Rose." His lips lingered over her forehead as he leaned down and bestowed a kiss across her brow.

Rosalind sighed happily. "Goodnight, my barbarian..."

He laughed.

"My Norse god," she added with a blush.

His smile was so wide it hurt. "Goodnight."

CHAPTER THIRTEEN

Sleep that knits up the ravelled sleave of care
The death of each day's life, sore labour's bath
Balm of hurt minds, great nature's second course,
Chief nourisher in life's feast.
~ Macbeth — William Shakespeare ~

STEFAN AWOKE WITH A crick in his back and an all around horrid premonition that today would not be a good day. For one thing, when he went to see to Samson, he discovered his horse had been busy all night eating. And was now moving slower than normal.

Rosalind had awoken looking fresher than a spring flower. He had every intention of asking her to marry him. Of waking her with flowers and sonnets, things she deserved. That he wanted to give her. But, after he saddled Samson, it was discovered that both Alfred and Mary were missing.

Imagine his surprise when he caught them both leaving the stables at the same time. Mary with straw in her hair, and dare he say Alfred with more pomp in his step than he had seen in all his years.

His mind didn't allow him to think about what had been transpiring between the two, though he had a notion to scold them for being so... careless. Then again, that could have been jealousy talking.

He'd never woke so physically wound with desire. It made matters much more difficult than he could imagine now that he realized his heart was very much involved. Unable to decipher between his lust and suspicions of love for the woman, he found himself incapable of making sound decisions. So he rode the carriage in silence, all the while watching Rosalind for any indication that she was thinking of him too. Instead, she stared out the window as if the bloody horizon was the most interesting thing she'd ever set eyes on.

Out of curiosity he looked, but saw nothing save the snow and dreary country side.

Was he not better to look at? Curse his pride that continued to go missing on such occasions!

Finally, as a last resort, he reached across the carriage and grasped Rosalind's hand, much to Mary's disgust. He hadn't time to even enjoy the feeling of her feminine hand because he was too blasted busy watching Mary while she continued to thump her cane. Sweating profusely by the time they reached the townhome, he was never more thankful to be done with a carriage ride in his life.

Rosalind's hand continued to tingle long after Stefan released it to help her out of the carriage. Odd, her mind was more focused on the simple object of his hand more so than her mother's sickness. But to be quite honest she hadn't been focused on her mother at all. Not now, and not last night when she was alone with the very man she had been turning down for the past three days.

Sighing, she looked to Mary for strength, but she was already on her way into the house, Stefan's valet close behind. Odd, Alfred appeared to have straw in his coat?

Rosalind shook her head and continued her journey up the stairs into her home; she hadn't been back in London since her father's death. The house looked the same, a large white mansion in the stylish part of Grosvenor square. Though the grounds appeared to look gloomier than before, and made Rosalind wonder just how destitute the new earl had left her family.

Straightening her dress, she readied herself to take a step then felt Stefan's hand on the small of her back, urging her forward. She shot him a nervous glance. He winked and increased the pressure, forcing her to take the few steps into her old home.

Why was she trembling? As the butler opened the door, her senses were overwhelmed with the familiar smell of dusty books, from her father's expansive library and the overwhelming scent of beeswax.

To his credit, Stefan didn't say a word at the scarcity of the house though Rosalind knew he was probably curious. How could he not be? For upon their entry no servants greeted them. The residual feeling of her father was still present as though no one wanted to admit he was gone. Shaking, she walked to her father's old study and opened the door. Dust gave her a warm welcome. In her grief, her mother must have sanctioned the room off.

"Come," Stefan called behind her. "We should see to your mother. Do you think you can lead me to her rooms?"

Rosalind wasn't sure she wanted to see her mother. The very same mother that blamed her for her father's death even though she had done nothing to cause it.

She looked to the sofa where she had sat months before

cradling her dads head as he breathed his last breath. His hand cupping her cheek, a tear running down his weathered face. By the time the doctor had arrived, her mother had escorted her to her rooms and informed her that if she didn't marry the curse would surely take them all. Rosalind left the very next day and never looked back. It was also the same day her doctor had said that he could do nothing for her sleeping episodes other than wait for it to kill her. His thoughts were that anything that caused one to fall asleep at odd times would surely progress until one day she didn't wake up.

Weakening, she reached for something to lean onto as the pain of that day washed over her.

"Rosalind, we can see to your mother later. Do you need a minute?" Stefan's warm breath fanned at her face. As the smell of lye and cinnamon drifted off him, Rosalind couldn't help herself as she turned into his arms and wept. Stefan didn't stiffen, nor did he move away or tell her to compose herself. He simply wrapped his large arms around her and caressed her hair.

When she was finally able to stop sniffling, embarrassment washed over her. She tensed, but he didn't allow her to pull away instead his lips tickled her ear in a whisper. "Embarrassment is not necessary when one grieves the loss of a parent dear to them, Rosalind. Death is a natural part of life, but a terrible beast when it suddenly knocks on ones door. Never harden your heart to the God-given emotions that help us heal most, sweetheart."

Stefan's lips brushed her forehead in a chaste kiss. Instinctively, she wrapped her arms around his waist and nodded, unable to get out words.

Minutes later, she pulled back and looked into his concerned eyes. "I believe I'm ready."

Nodding, he moved away from her and allowed her to lead them out of the study and up the marble staircase to the second floor.

Rosalind was still shocked to see no servants scurrying about. As she came to her mother's door she knocked and then opened it.

Her mother was sitting on her bed fully clothed reading with a glass of sherry in hand. "Gwendolyn, if that's you then I've told you already I don't need any more blankets, I'm just fine the way I am. It is merely the sniffles!"

Rosalind gasped unable to hide her excitement that her mother was in fact the picture of health. "Oh, I am so relieved!"

The countess looked up and paled. "Rosalind? Oh, um. You came so soon my dear! I did not expect you until tomorrow at least!"

Her mother looked around her as if she wasn't at all excited to see her eldest daughter. Disappointment clouded her features as she looked from her to Stefan and then her nostrils flared. "I take it you are both married? Considering, it simply isn't done to travel alone on such short notice and I will not have my daughter ruined by your reckless ways, Your Grace."

"Married?" Rosalind swallowed the guilty lump in her throat. "Mama, we didn't need to marry. I had Mary travel along with us."

"Mary? Your godmother, Mary?" Her mother spat venomously. "She has been under strict orders to stay at the estate in Sussex until I call upon her to return!" Her mother folded her hands across her chest, clearly reeling.

"Are you well, Mother?"

"Of course I'm not well! My daughter hasn't lifted the curse, I have no servants to speak of considering we are only left with a pittance from the new earl and you brought *him* into our house!"

Rosalind flinched as the word *him* flew out of her

mother's mouth like an expletive. Stefan didn't move, nor did he curse. He merely took a step closer to Rosalind and placed his hands on her shoulders. Pulling strength from his presence — my how she had been doing a lot of that lately — she looked into her mother's cold eyes.

"It isn't up to you when we marry mother. Besides, he hasn't yet asked." She lied hoping Stefan would go along with it. She felt his hands clench her shoulders, was he trembling? The cad was trying not to laugh!

"Yes, well." Stefan's silky voice said behind her. "My apologies, madam. It seems I simply haven't been able to get the words right. Each time I begin my proposal it's as if it isn't good enough and I must try again. I must admit to being a coward when it comes to redheads."

Her mother glared even more looking between the two of them as if she was missing something. "Yes, well." She put down her book and sighed. "The curse will take us all if neither of you are quick about this business."

"You have a cold, mother. I hardly think that is the work of the some sort of ancient spell." Rosalind said as kind as she could without smiling.

"You think this funny, my gel? Have you no respect for the dead!" The room went silent. "If you cannot marry to save me or your sister, at least marry to honor your father's last wish, or did he mean nothing to you?"

"Watch yourself, my lady." Stefan tensed behind Rosalind. She willed him to back down, hoping he would not make things more difficult.

A man cleared his throat, breaking the tense silence after Stefan's announcement.

Rosalind looked to the door and smiled. "Willard! It is so good to see you after such a long time!" Her father's old valet had apparently stayed on staff. The familiar look of his old face made Rosalind want to weep all over again. The man nodded at her and then looked to Stefan with a calculating glare.

"I see that congratulations are in order," he said, not taking his eyes from Stefan's.

"Well actually, we did not have need to marry just yet Willard."

The valet's mouth pursed into a thin hard line. "So you are not married yet, my lady? Well, this changes things, now doesn't it? I imagine the rest of your family will continue to die, as well as the servants." He backed out of the room, but stopped when Stefan's voice boomed after him.

"What do you mean the rest of the servants?"

Willard looked to Rosalind's mother for permission. At her nod, he looked back to Stefan. "Two of the young chamber maids have been ill. Both have symptoms of a sleeping disease. It takes them at inopportune times during the day, making it difficult for them to complete tasks. We've seen doctors. It is inexplicable. We imagine death will take them as it took my master."

Rosalind's heart stopped beating. The girls had her sickness? Did that mean it was contagious? Then the doctor was correct. She would surely die. Was it because of the curse? Or was it merely a coincidence?

"Daughter, you look quite ill. Are *you* well?" Her mother gave a cruel smile in her direction. "You must be tired. Why don't you take a nap? Willard has some lovely tea he can give you. You remember the type? You used to drink it daily as a child."

Rosalind's feet were glued to the floor. Unable to do anything except look into her mother's cruel eyes. A face filled with pain and bitterness. How had her family come to this?

"Where's Isabelle?" Rosalind's voice was weak.

"Around. The girl is such a disappointment, crying in her room daily because of her father's death, while I'm sitting here lamenting the selfish daughter I raised who refuses to do this one thing! But of course, I'm sure Isabelle would love to hear your important reasons for not marrying, my dear."

"Excuse me." Rosalind swept out of the room; blindly she walked down the hall not knowing in which direction to go. Warm salty tears streamed down her face. Strong arms pulled her out of the hallway.

"Tsk, tsk, Rose. We can't have you crying anymore. You don't want me thinking I can use your sadness to my advantage by seducing you out of the doldrums."

Even as Stefan spoke the words, his hands were gentle as he pushed fallen hair from her face and tilted her chin upwards with his warm hand.

"A moment of weakness." Rosalind managed a smile. "She seems to be getting more horrid with age."

"Your mother?"

She nodded.

"Yes well, I thought she was lovely. Only twice did I contemplate choking that neck of hers, and I had half a mind to pat myself on the back for my restraint."

Rosalind laughed, covering her mouth with her hands at Stefan's obvious attempt to pull her out of the melancholy she was in.

"What?" he asked, looking offended. "Don't tell me you weren't thinking the exact same thing, little minx. Now, let us straighten you up." His thumbs wiped the tears from her eyes. "There we go, now you look like the same redhead that told me my sonnet was stupid and my proposals lacking."

Rosalind bit her lip against the hammering of her heart.

Stefan's hand reached up. Taking her by surprise he pulled at the back of her head and kissed her so hard she thought she may expire on the spot. His tongue dove into her mouth without restraint. Large hands twisted into her hair and tugged her entire body forward.

He pulled back with a smug grin. "Aw, there's that fire I'm so used to. Glad to see you set to rights again. Shall we?" He opened the door and offered his arm.

Insufferable man! She didn't know whether to pull him back into the room and beg of him to kiss her again or slap him for his advances. In fact, she wasn't even sure how her wobbly legs managed to move in a straight line. The man was an emotional complexity! How was it that he was able to offer her sound advice in the same breath he used to kiss her senseless?

Cursing the man for his seduction abilities that she earlier mocked, she made her way with Stefan in tow towards her younger sister's room.

"Aghhhhh!" A scream erupted from her mother's rooms.

Panicking, Rosalind turned on her heel and ran. Stefan was ahead of her and in the room before she was able.

"What the devil happened here?" he roared.

Rosalind gasped when she came into the room. Her mother was lying on her side motionless and pale.

"Is she…" Rosalind shuddered.

Willard was next to her side, his face contorted with rage. "She seems to have developed similar symptoms to the other maids. She said she was in pain so I brought her some tea, then she complained of stomach cramps and fell into a deep sleep it seems."

"Call for the doctor immediately," Stefan ordered.

Willard merely stood there motionless before adding. "Your Grace, pardon my outspokenness, but we've been dealing with this cursed disease for the past few weeks. A doctor will not help. She will slowly go mad. I'm sure of it."

"I said…" Stefan clenched his fists. "Call for the doctor."

"Your Grace." Willard gave a curt bow and exited the room.

"Well, it appears my family has gone mad." Rosalind

looked at her mother's motionless form.

"Rose, I hate to say this now, and I know my proposals haven't been the stuff of legends, but..."

A heavy weight of guilt descended onto her shoulders. Maybe they were right, she was being selfish. How morose of a thought — to know that she would surely die married to a man she was starting to care for. The thought that she was actually developing feelings for Stefan didn't aid her confusion. It caused her heart great pain. Even worse than his botched proposals was the fact that she was hiding the seriousness of her health issues from his very astute eyes. He knew nothing of the constant fear that plagued her. The horrible premonition that one day, she would simply fall asleep and never wake up.

"What are you saying, Stefan?"

"Rose, if it is the curse..." he didn't finish the sentence; he didn't need to. The house felt constricting and all at once frightening and cold. His eyes landed on her mother's frail form.

"Are you still in possession of the special license, Stefan?"

After a moment of silence, he said, "I am."

Rosalind closed her eyes. She had to make the decision without looking at her mother's still form and pale face. "Of course you are. Always dependable. We shall marry in two days. That will give me adequate time to make arrangements."

"As you wish." His voice was barely audible. Was he regretting the hastiness of their marriage? Or was he merely trying to be humble about her decision?

She would never know, for the next minute her world turned on its ear as a very pale woman ran into the room and announced. "They are both dead! The two maids, my friends... they are dead!"

CHAPTER FOURTEEN

I am tainted whether of the flock,
Meetest for death: the weakest kind of fruit
Drops earliest to the ground.
~ The Merchant of Venice — William Shakespeare ~

STEFAN WAS ALREADY ON his third snifter of brandy when the doctor was gathering his things to leave the house. He hadn't even been to see his own family, considering Rosalind's had already driven him to drink. He didn't feel the need to add to the mind-consuming madness that had taken place since his arrival in London.

"Your Grace?" The doctor poked his head into the library where Stefan was drowning his nerves.

"You may enter," he motioned. "And how is the dowager this evening?"

The doctor looked away, put up a hand, then walked to the door and closed it. "Your Grace, if I may speak plainly?"

"Please do so."

"How much do you know of the late earl and his wife?"

Stefan shifted uncomfortably in his seat before taking another sip of brandy. "I know that the late earl died of heart failure and that the entire family, as well as mine, believes some sort of curse is killing off our family trees one by one until I marry the eldest daughter."

"I cannot speak for the curse." The doctor swallowed slowly his eyes downcast, "but the late earl was a good man. A finer friend I could not ask for. What I find strange, Your Grace, is that we had an understanding. His health was declining, we were both aware that his heart was weak, but I had just seen him the day previous and he was healthier than I had seen him look in years."

"What, exactly are you saying?" Stefan leaned forward.

"I do not believe he died of natural causes, Your Grace."

"Have you any evidence or is this merely your opinion?" Stefan asked swirling the amber liquid around.

"He was drinking, Your Grace."

"And that proves your hypothesis how?" Stefan could not help the shudder that took over his body. Something was odd in this house. And the doctor's doubts only added to his own.

"He did not drink, Your Grace."

"Ever?"

"Not since his diagnosis. I would say he had not a drop of alcohol for at least two years."

"And how do you know he was drinking, doctor?"

The doctor began pacing. "When I arrived, he was already dead. And the scene before me was heartbreaking to say the least. There was so much commotion I almost missed it. But next to his chair by the fireplace I noticed a sniffer of brandy. Nothing out of the ordinary, but it was only half full and had been tipped over."

"That does not prove much." Stefan admitted.

"I am merely telling you what I've observed." The doctor

stopped pacing. "Maybe my grief is talking. The good Lord knows only the daughters have grieved that loss."

Stefan didn't feel it was his place to ask what the doctor was referring to. He stored the information in the back of his mind as the doctor continued talking.

"As if things could not get any more peculiar. I find nothing wrong with the Dowager."

"Nothing?" Stefan asked aghast.

"Absolutely nothing. She's sleeping. Nothing more. Albeit, it is a strong sleep. Most likely drug induced, although I do not know why she would do such a thing."

"Thank you, doctor." Stefan rose from his seat and pumped the man's hand. "And I will think on what you've said."

"Thank you."

The doctor went to the door, but as he reached for it, it swung open wide revealing Willard. "Oh, good sir, I was just coming to fetch you. The hackney is here."

The doctor nodded and walked off, leaving Stefan alone with the alarming news of the doctor's discovery. Something was taking place in this household. And he was going to find out what.

Rosalind. She should at least know if her father was drinking brandy or behaving out of sorts. She had seen him in his last moments. Should he bring back those painful memories though?

It was decided for him as Rosalind entered the room minutes later searching for a book.

"Oh, Stefan. I'm sorry, I knew I would have trouble sleeping so I came in search of a book, but I can come back at another time."

"Wait." He stood nearly knocking the brandy in his hand over in all his haste. "Stay, please."

Rosalind looked towards the door then back at him. She

must have decided she would rather spend time talking with him than tossing and turning in her bed, for she came near him and sat, tucking her feet beneath her.

"Brandy?" he offered.

Smiling, she nodded her head. Who wouldn't need brandy after a day like today? If he stayed much longer in this madhouse he'd be a perpetual drunk.

He poured her a glass and handed it over.

She sniffed it before taking a large swallow.

"Rose, your mother…" How does one tell news such as this? Sorry, but your mother's insane?

"She's the devil." Rosalind cursed and threw back the rest of her drink. Well yes, one could always be blunt. His little Rose, always honest to a fault.

"Well, yes there is that. Stole the words right from my mouth. Granted, I had others to add in as well. Colorful words too, would you like to hear them?"

Rosalind laughed. "Maybe after another drink." She held out her glass. "I have half a mind to tell Samson to trample her."

"He'd listen to you too. The cursed horse likes you better than he likes me, though he has revulsion of getting his hooves too dirty. I imagine he would somehow convince another horse to do his dirty work, all the while eating oats in the stable."

Rosalind laughed loud and deep, causing Stefan's blood to stir. "My groom is positively enamored of that horse. I'll be surprised if he can even move after all the food he's been consuming."

"Glutton." Stefan chuckled then sobered as Rosalind looked away with watery eyes.

"Rose… I spoke with the doctor."

"As did I," she admitted eyes still watery. "It appears she will stop at nothing to hurt me. I just don't understand why she would cause such an uproar when she isn't even ill."

"Boredom?" Stefan offered. "Or maybe she wants to cause you pain for not abiding by her wishes. Regardless, we should keep a close eye on her." Stefan's mind went back to the odd mannerisms of the valet. "And the servants as well." The ones who were still alive that is. What a mess.

Rosalind sighed, drinking her brandy in silence. "Did the doctor say anything else?"

His opportunity could not have been better. "Actually," he set his glass down and leaned forward drawing courage from the burn of the alcohol down his throat. "I was wondering about your father."

"Oh?"

"Yes, was he drinking the night he died, Rosalind? I know it is painful to talk about, but the doctor has suspicions, and I am merely trying to ascertain the truth to prove or disprove his theories."

Rosalind nibbled on her lower lip distracting Stefan from his line of questioning. Rather than thinking about the odd happenings of the day, he found himself daydreaming about the taste of her lips and the feel of them as he slipped his tongue past her defenses.

"He was!" she blurted, stunning him out of his erotic dream.

"Drinking, you mean?" he asked.

"Yes! I know for certain because I thought he might be drunk, he was mumbling to himself when I walked into his study, but he had slowly been deteriorating. He put his glass on the ground and approached me and when he fell, well he must have knocked it over, for I don't recall seeing it after the incident. Perhaps they cleaned it up after the doctor left."

"Yes, perhaps." Stefan didn't think it wise to share his suspicions with Rosalind. "Where do you wish to marry?" he changed the subject as best he could. "I believe we can secure a church in this short amount of time. It will be nice to have our families present now, won't it?"

"I suppose, though I still haven't laid eyes on either of my sisters; one would think they were missing or something." Rosalind shrugged and offered a smile. "Are we doing the right thing, Stefan?"

Leave it to her to ask the logical question. "The right thing for our families? Yes, sweetheart, we are."

"And for us?" She quickly looked down and began swirling the remains of her brandy.

He took the glass from her hand and walked around the desk taking a stand in front of her. Stefan reached out his hand and brought her to her feet. "I can only speak for myself." He watched as she licked her lips and leaned forward. "Selfishly, I would marry you regardless of the curse, Rosalind, and that's the truth. Though you can imagine I would make a larger spectacle of myself. The sonnets would of course be written better than Byron himself. I'd throw rocks at your bedroom window in hopes that you'd let me up. And since being slightly foxed demands brutal honesty, I'll admit to trying to seduce you every day until the vows were said."

Green eyes widened as she gave as light sigh.

"Surprised?" he asked huskily.

"Not really." She grinned.

His control snapped. Like a hungry lion he swept in and devoured her mouth with all the force of emotion he had been keeping in throughout the night. With a moan, she wrapped her arms around his neck and pulled him into her embrace. It was as if a fight of desperation had broken free, for she frantically pulled at his jacket until it was off of his shoulders, and he in return tugged at her hair until it was free of pins.

Her once passive participation was suddenly aggressive, and Stefan found it hard to keep up with her enthusiasm as he was trying to think of a way to remove her clothes and happily possess her without wasting too much time. His need to protect her fought with his desire to bed her. A fierce battle for control raged within his chest. The last thing he wanted to be was reasonable as her fists grabbed a hold of his unfashionably long hair.

He cursed himself. In all these years, it would be now that he would develop a conscience and push the girl away only to spend the night in a frightful sleep of need.

"Rose." He pulled away. "Sweetheart." He grabbed at her hands still clenched within his hair and brought them to his lips. "Believe me when I say I want nothing more than to take you right here in the library without a care for who sees or how it looks." He glanced at her swollen lips. "To the devil with propriety."

She laughed, her eyes glistening with need. "Yet," he caressed her face. "I find that I would not be able to live with myself if I took what was not mine in a fit of passion brought on by heightened emotions and a trying day. Please forgive me for being strong when I so desperately wish to be weak."

"For a brute, that was quite poetic." Rosalind said as a blush crept up her cheeks. "Does this mean you're saving your weakness for me and only me, Your Grace?"

His heart began thudding wildly. "But of course. I imagine I'll have plenty of weakness stored up for our wedding night. The only question is, will you be up for it or expire on the spot with your own delicate sensibilities?"

Rosalind lifted an eyebrow as she playfully jerked her hands free of his grasp. "Oh, Stefan, you should know me better by now."

"Pardon?"

Gathering her skirts she walked slowly towards the door and spoke without turning around. "I am anything but delicate."

His body begged and pleaded for him to race after her, to

slam the door in her face and push her body up against it. He had to close his eyes to fight the emotions swelling within him. Stefan was truly worried that he wouldn't make it. An insane godmother with aversions to pink, a suspicious valet, an enraged mother, a temptress, and a horse that acted more like a person than an animal. If he walked away without going mad, he would count himself fortunate.

Later on in the evening, his body fought for control. Part of him demanded he find Rosalind's rooms and finish what they started. The other half told him to find sleep in any way possible.

Neither won, which come morning left him in a foul mood. It did nothing to help matters that on impulse he had slept in the library in order to protect Rosalind. At least that was what he told himself, though he wondered if he was more worried about himself attacking her or her mother. Most likely, it was a tie, leaving him again aggravated.

He pulled at his shirtsleeves and managed to make himself presentable before jumping into his carriage and making haste for his own home, leaving a note that he would return to Rosalind within a few hours once he was presentable.

Nothing sounded better than a good night's rest and a strong cup of tea. He could almost feel his bed and taste the bitter brew on his lips as he took the steps two at a time to his London townhome in Mayfair.

He lifted his hand to knock just as the door swung open.

"Stefan?" His brother James looked alarmed. "Whatever are you doing here? Have you failed in some way?"

Grinding his teeth against the urge to pummel his brother for asking so many questions at such an early hour, Stefan merely shook his head in a grunt and pushed his brother aside. His luggage was brought in hastily and somewhat clumsily. He knew he could at least sleep one hour before having to ready for the day and return to Rosalind's before her mother got any notion to eat her young.

CHAPTER FIFTEEN

The course of true love never did run smooth.
~ A Midsummer Night's Dream ~

ROSALIND WOKE AT AN early hour after a fitful night of sleep. It was astonishing that she felt as rested as she did. Looking in the mirror at her still swollen lips, her thoughts drifted towards Stefan, her soon to be husband. How she desperately had wanted him to take away all the doubt and fear that consumed her thoughts enough to force her to seek solitude in the library. Instead, he had done the honorable thing.

It appeared she was wrong about many things, Stefan included. Yes, he was arrogant and at times an absolute brute, but when it counted — when she really needed a shoulder to cry on, or comforting words, he was there.

Rosalind performed her morning toilette briskly and went in search of her sisters. They were as unalike as any siblings could be. The youngest, Isabelle had chestnut hair, blue eyes, and was a petite little thing. Everyone who met her immediately fell in love with her sweet disposition. Rosalind's mother had often fought with Rosalind over the fact that she was so blunt and stubborn. Her mother's desire was for Rosalind to be more like Isabelle. It just wasn't in Rosalind's character to be that way.

Gwendolyn, the middle daughter had long dark hair that fell in waves down her back. She was the envy of woman everywhere simply because her skin was so fair it gave off the illusion of a pearl. She had ice blue eyes and a dangerous smile, but often kept to herself. It was Rosalind who had been launched first. Her sisters were stowed away at the family estate until it was time for their debut. It seemed everything was put on pause since her father's death. Rosalind couldn't help but wonder if things would be different if he were still alive.

Hallways once filled with laughter were void of human touch. Dust floated into the air as Rosalind made her way to her sisters' bedrooms. She stopped outside Isabelle's door and knocked.

"Enter," came a small voice from inside.

Rosalind pushed open the door and gasped. Isabelle, was sitting near the fireplace with Gwendolyn on one side of her brushing out the long chestnut hair.

"Sisters!" Rosalind ran to them expecting them to politely stare at her, they hadn't spoken since her father's death. Her mother had poisoned them against her ever since the broken betrothal contract was severed, leaving her even more estranged from her family than she ever thought possible.

"Rosalind!" Isabelle jumped from her seat and threw her arms around her waist. "You've come home! Isn't it wonderful, Gwen?"

Gwendolyn smiled and walked over to the pair a tear running down her cheek. "I wished for your return every day, sister. Tell me you are well."

Rosalind thought about telling the truth but hadn't her

sisters suffered enough? Swallowing the lie, she smiled. "I'm better than I've ever been! And I'm to be married!"

"Married?" They said in unison.

"To whom?" Gwen spoke up first.

Rosalind grinned as memories of Stefan's kiss came flooding back. "To the Duke of Montmouth."

Isabelle paled. "Does mother know then? That you intend to marry him and break the curse?"

"Yes, of course, why?" Rosalind shrugged.

Isabelle's eyes flickered to Gwen then back to Rosalind. "She hasn't been well since you left Rose. We fear, well we fear something is amiss. We've been prisoners in our own home it seems. The servants are gone. There is hardly food on the table. We were left with nothing. To make matters worse Willard won't let us see her but a few hours a day, and after she drinks that blasted tea she sleeps for days."

Gwen cursed. "That Dominique stole everything from us, he's a beast!

Isabelle patted her sister's hand. "Gwen, we don't know for sure if he's doing it purposefully or if he is even aware of our destitution just yet." She turned towards Rosalind. "The only information we gain is from mother, when she feels like lamenting, that is." Both sisters looked down at their hands as if keeping another grand secret from Rosalind.

"What would you have me do?" Rosalind asked weakly. "Once I marry Stefan, we'll sort things out. We can move to his country seat."

Isabelle grabbed Rosalind's hand. "I just hope it is all in time, dear sister. For I can't help the feeling of foreboding I receive every time mother looks at me. It's as if she plans something horrible."

Rosalind squeezed her hand back. "Let's not get ahead of ourselves. There is to be a winter ball tonight. Shall we plan for that with excitement?"

The girls looked at her with sadness in their eyes. "Rose," Gwen started. "We don't have the funds to obtain gowns nice enough to—"

"There you are." Stefan stepped into the room, followed by a very put out butler who seemed about ready to pull pistols on the intrusive duke. His large presence stole the breath straight from Rosalind's lungs. "Your Grace." She did a little curtsy and nodded to her sisters who merely stood ramrod straight, mouths gaping. It wasn't at all proper for him to be in their chambers, but nothing about Stefan was proper. Duke or no duke, she imagined that if he decided he suddenly wanted to become king he would find a way to do it.

Glancing at her sisters and their shocked expressions, she tried to imagine what Stefan would look like through new eyes. Tall, broad, and graced with more elegance than any man she had ever met. It was no wonder her two sisters stared at him as if a Norse god had just walked into their chambers. His Hessians were shined to perfection, a tailored jacket around his broad shoulders and a perfectly tied cravat. His blond hair was tucked behind his ears and a cane in hand. He was the epitome of masculine beauty.

Rosalind bit back a smile. A sort of protectiveness washed over her as she realized how proud she was to be a part of his life. He did a short bow to both her sisters and approached Rosalind. Her heart beat wildly as her eyes locked onto his lips.

Leaning down, he grabbed her hand and brushed his lips across her fingers but not before she felt the hot intrusion of his tongue against her skin. Flushing, she pulled back in time to see him wink before wrapping a possessive arm around her.

"Now, what's this I hear about dresses and a ball?"

Fuming, the butler mumbled something to himself and marched out of the room. Stefan glanced in his direction as if he were an annoying fly needing to be shuffled out of the room and shrugged. His full attention was now back on the three women.

"It's nothing, Your Grace, really—" Isabelle was shaking her head.

"Don't be absurd. I believe a shopping trip is in order, is it not? I have a carriage waiting to take you three girls wherever your heart desires. An early wedding gift for Rose. Find some suitable dresses that can be hastily made, and we will all attend the ball tonight."

Rosalind was without words. She closed her eyes against the intrusion of confusing feelings hammering in her heart. This courtship was much easier when she was in her country estate telling the infuriating man to woo her while he had split pea soup on his chin. Now, his generosity and kisses were enough to make her dizzy.

"We could not possibly accept." Gwen gave Rosalind a questioning look. And it seemed that Rosalind saw her sister's apparel for the first time. Both wore simple muslin dresses, a little frayed around the bottom edges and not the current style that was en vogue. She looked down at her own dress and flushed. How could she have forgotten about such a thing as their current state of dress? If things were truly as her sisters said, then there was no possible way they could attend a ball with current gowns they owned, regardless of the season being over.

Isabelle's hopeful eyes trained on Rosalind, and she found she was too weak to do anything except nod her head and squeeze Stefan's hand. His brisk squeeze back sent butterflies from her stomach to her toes.

"I'll just leave you ladies to it then. I'll be avoiding your mother and that awful valet by waiting in the carriage. It seems Samson needs some attention considering he kicked open the gate to his stable last night and made his way to the large feeder containing oats." He shook his head. "Surprised the blasted horse hasn't died from over-indulgence."

Rosalind laughed and felt the need to explain. "His horse is… temperamental, to say the least."

Isabelle smiled. "Is he at all like Felipe?"

Rosalind had forgotten all about her sister's giant horse. "Yes, too much like Felipe. My only hope is that they don't join forces."

"Don't hold your breath," Stefan muttered. "Ladies, I'll be waiting."

He quit the room in long even strides and shut the door behind him. Rosalind's eyes were still trained on the closed door as memories of his touch came flooding back.

"Dear sister, I believe you're blushing," Gwen teased.

"I'm merely…" Rosalind cursed her inability to find the right lie, or words to excuse her odd behavior.

"Flushing dear, you're flushed." Isabelle said helpfully. "Now, let us don our bonnets so we can be on our way. I haven't shopped in an age, and I cannot wait to visit Bond Street! Do you think the duke will allow us a short jaunt to the book store as well?"

Rosalind gave her youngest sister a warm smile. "I'm sure if you ask sweetly enough and feed Samson oats, the duke will agree to just about anything."

Gwen huffed. "But just to be safe, we'll allow Rosalind to do all the talking. It seems to distract the brute long enough to get away with a multitude of sins."

Rosalind really didn't have any response to the blatant truth flowing from her sister's mouth. Shrugging, she helped them find their bonnets and let out a sigh as she thought about the upcoming ball.

Stefan counted every step he took as he made his way to

the stables in search of Samson. The groom, having already put up with Samson the previous night uttered a sigh of relief when he saw the duke make his way towards the horse.

Samson neighed irritably and Stefan found his mood exactly matched his horses, not that it was any grand revelation.

His purpose on arriving after only receiving two hours of sleep was to tell Rosalind of the strange happenings at his home, but every serious thought left him the minute he set eyes on her. And he found he was more inclined to help her and her sisters than cause them more panic than necessary.

After all, he hadn't any proof that the strange happenings were connected. It just seemed… odd. His brother James had informed him that his mother was beginning to show signs of the mysterious illness that had plagued Fitz. The dowager was often times tired and short of breath keeping to her bed most days. James however didn't seem ill at all but the dark circles under his eyes proved that he too felt the pressure from the curse or whatever else was happening in his family.

"What do you intend to do?" James had asked him.

"Marry her and be done with it." Stefan hadn't meant to sound so harsh but was losing patience in the presence of his insipid brother.

James looked away before answering in a low trembling voice, "It will solve nothing brother, absolutely nothing."

Stefan's hair stood on end as his brother left the room. What did he mean? On cue Elaina, Fitz's wife, burst onto the scene.

"He's worsening! But there isn't any explanation! He only drinks his tea and barely touches his food!"

"Tea?" Stefan looked at the woman he once thought beautiful and perfect, indignation rising in his chest over the hurt Fitz must feel at her betrayal. "Fitz despises tea."

"It's said to have healing properties, just last week Mr.

Fairbanks said it was helping his mistress as well."

"Mr. Fairbanks?" Stefan searched his mind, why did the name sound so familiar. "Who is his mistress?"

"The Dowager Countess of Hariss, of course." Elaina answered curtly.

Stefan shook his head and patted Samson on the neck. Why would that strange valet Willard make a visit to their house? Naturally, if he knew they were all suffering from the same sickness he would want to help. But why did Stefan feel like help was the last thing Mr. Willard Fairbanks wanted to offer?

Footsteps neared crunching against the grass and stopped. He whipped around to see Rosalind standing before him. A bonnet covering her vibrant hair.

"I wanted to say thank you." Her eyes dropped to the ground.

Stefan chuckled. "To the dirt or to me? Apologies for my confusion, but it seems when one says thank you they do so by looking at the object they are thanking."

He noticed her swallow, watched as her neck slowly lifted that downcast head until her eyes met his in a compassionate stare. "Stefan, I…"

Enjoying her discomfort, he folded his arms around his chest and tilted his head to the side. "You…"

"I was wrong."

"Sorry love, what was that?"

Glaring, she fisted both hands and walked closer to where he stood. "I was wrong. I know how difficult this must be for you to understand, considering you rarely apologize, but that is exactly what I'm doing."

"And you were doing such an admirable job before you allowed your passionate side to get in the way, weren't you, Rose?"

Her eyes darted away. He turned her head to face his,

unapologetic about his grip on her chin as he drew her near and brushed a kiss across her lips.

"What were you wrong about, Rose?"

She stiffened. "Anyone can see us out here."

"Let them," he growled. "Now, let's hear the apology, shall we?"

Her eyes sparked. "Fine then. You aren't nearly as barbaric as I once thought, nor do you have the manners of an ogre."

"You never called me an ogre."

"Out loud, I didn't." She smiled, "And when it counts..." Her lower lip trembled. "...when I need someone, something stable, the only image my mind can conjure up is one of you."

Samson neighed and nudged Rosalind in the thigh. "And Samson, of course." She added now giving full attention to the horse as she ran her kid gloves along his white fur.

Stefan glared at his horse and silently conveyed a message of a land without oats void of any trots and filled with nothing, save geldings. Samson, didn't seem to notice the look of disapproval on his master's face and merely rubbed against Rosalind all the more.

"Bloody animal," Stefan stepped in between the two and grabbed Rosalind by the shoulders. "I care about you a great deal, Rose. I—"

"—Are you two ready?" Isabelle came around the corner with her sister in tow. "It's late in the morning, and we need time to find gowns and prepare!"

Words of love hung in the air. Would he never get his opportunity to tell her how he felt? With a shake he nodded his head, "Of course."

The girls turned and giggled. Rosalind ran ahead to join them. All three of their little heads together in excitement.

His face took on a smile that nearly hurt from its expansiveness, and Samson nudged him quite hard on the backside, as if to say, "Don't be an idiot."

"Helpful," Stefan muttered and followed the girls to the awaiting carriage, but not before stopping and giving the groom strict instructions to hide the oats. He left the stables with noises of Samson's protests. That'll teach him to try to steal his future duchess.

CHAPTER SIXTEEN

One may smile and smile, and be a villain!
~ Hamlet ~

THAT NIGHT AS ROSALIND looked in the mirror at her silk ball gown, she let out a giggle of delight. She hadn't been to a ball since the night of Stefan's re-appearance into society. Her nerves were on edge but only because the last time she was at a ball, she had promptly fallen asleep under one of the spells that so often plagued her. Mayhap the sickness was leaving her. Doctors were proven wrong all the time, weren't they? And she hadn't had a spell for months!

She took a sip of tea that Willard had brought and exhaled as she donned her new gloves and went in search of her sisters.

Stefan was waiting at the bottom of stairs looking more like a duke than she had ever seen him. Shuddering with delight at his devil may care smile, she felt herself flush as she met him at the bottom of the stairs.

"One more day," he said as he kissed her hand.

"Pardon?"

His eyes raked her up and down. "I'll allow your imagination to finish the sentiment."

Before she could swat him for his rakish attitude, her sisters descended the stairs giggling in excitement. They were beautiful. Isabelle was in a light yellow that brought out her warm features and Gwen was in an off-white that set off her red rose lips and dark hair to perfection.

"Shall we, ladies?" Stefan announced holding out his arm to Rosalind. They all nodded and followed him out to the ducal carriage.

As they were announced at the ball, Rosalind could not help but wince as people began whispering immediately. No doubt, they were all privy to the rumors surrounding both families and the mysterious deaths that encumbered them.

"Pay them no mind." Stefan whispered. "Today you enter as a lady, tomorrow you will be received as a duchess."

Gaining strength from his words, Rosalind was able to nod and smile at those who would wish ill of her and talk about her.

"Grandmother," Stefan said as the dowager of Barlowe approached them with her jeweled hands extended. "Stefan! And look who is with you! Have I understood correctly that you both are to be married tomorrow?"

"Yes," Stefan said looking away. "It will be a short private ceremony we aren't inviting anyone, just merely want to be done with the whole business."

"Well, I never!" The dowager sputtered. "My dear, he is such a rakehell. Please forgive his misdeeds and marry him despite his foolishness." She turned back to Stefan, "And you!" She poked him in the chest. "A woman's wedding day is very important, how dare you say otherwise. I am appalled." With a shake of her head she walked off leaving Rosalind with the terrible problem of hiding her laughter from Stefan.

"Laugh all you want, the woman has no shame. She also seems to know everyone's secrets, though for the life of me I cannot figure out how. It appears she has ears everywhere. Be careful Rose, it seems the room is enchanted." He winked and led her to the refreshments.

Rosalind took in the expanse ballroom. It did in fact seem enchanted, whites and silvers were everywhere, the candlelight dancing on the walls and ceiling. A sudden chill washed over her. Why was her excitement always followed by foreboding?

Deciding that she needed to enjoy herself, she watched as several people nodded to her and stared at Stefan as if he was Adonis himself. It wasn't as big of a crush as normal. People seemed to be enjoying the food and drink more than usual as well. Debutantes weren't dancing in droves, and it seemed that every hallway was darkly lit, whereas during the season it was hard to make an escape.

"So you've decided to come back to us, is that it?" A masculine voice interrupted her thoughts.

Turning on her heel, she gasped and let out a laugh as Lord Rawlings bowed over her hand. "I imagine I should ask for a dance before my wife sees you and doesn't allow any of us the pleasure of your company."

With dark hair and bright eyes, the man had always been pleasurable to look at. But he was her dear friend, Abby's husband. And a better husband Rosalind had never seen. In all honesty, it was what made her heart sick when thinking of a forced marriage. For one moment, she wanted to know what it would be like to have a man look at her the way Rawlings looked at his wife.

"Shall we?" he asked, his hand outstretched.

As they twirled around the floor, Rosalind could not help but reflect on her first impression of the man. Dark, dangerous, and a rake at heart. His countenance was now different, happier, and more comfortable in his own skin than she had ever seen him. It also helped that women didn't throw reticules at his head anymore, but that was an entirely different story.

"Are you well, Lady Rosalind?" Rawlings turned, and joined hands with her again.

"As well as I can be. I'm to be married."

Rawlings smile vanished. "To whom?"

Suddenly shy and not at all confident she should be sharing her tale of woe, she shrugged. "The Duke of Montmouth."

"Ah, the barbarian lost at sea. Tell me, does he use utensils at the table or merely growl and chew his meat like a brute?"

"Both." Rosalind laughed. "But to be fair, he has been very good to me."

Lord Rawlings squinted, looking into her eyes with such seriousness that she felt the need to turn away. "And the state of your heart, Rosalind? Let us talk of that matter. Do you love him?"

Leave it to Rawlings, once the most notorious rake in all of London, to pose such a question. "I cannot seem to help my heart from doing so, yes."

"And does he reciprocate your affection?"

The dance was coming to an end, and Rosalind was suddenly feeling tired, as if lead was pouring into her slippers.

"I can only hope that one day he will."

Satisfied, Rawlings turned her once more and bowed over her gloved hand. "Then I won't kill him."

"Rawlings!" she scolded but noticed he wasn't at all joking. With a smile she curtsied. "There is no need for you to kill him."

"Yes, please don't kill him," a deep and sensual voice interrupted.

"Ah, the barbarian approaches." Rawlings flashed a grin and pumped Stefan's hand. "A very wise woman once told me that women rarely play fair. I hope you understand what you are getting yourself into."

"I believe I can handle myself."

"It wasn't your emotional state I was referring to." Rawlings flashed another serious glance at Rosalind and bowed. "Do come visit us during your stay. Abby would be very pleased."

"Of course, my lord."

Stefan cursed under his breath and pulled Rosalind from the edge of the dance floor, doing nothing to hide his jealous sneer. "Just what was the man getting at? Was he rude to you? Why are you smiling? Devil take it, Rose!"

"Why, are you jealous?"

"That's preposterous." Stefan swore than patted his head. "I'm merely trying to protect you. I know Lord Rawlings to be a good fellow, but I may not trust him as easily as you though. He was quite the notorious rake."

"He offered to kill you." Rosalind added cheerfully, thinking it would be quite interesting to see Stefan's color change to a purplish hue of rage.

"He what!" Stefan bellowed.

"Rose!" Isabelle approached in a hurry. "Rose, he's here."

"He?" Rosalind asked.

"Whom?" Stefan looked at Isabelle his curiosity obviously piqued as well as his color, perhaps she should be kinder to the man.

Isabelle blushed. "Domi—"

"—Dominique Makyslov, Earl of Hariss." A deep cultured voice interrupted them, and Rosalind found herself wanting to kick Isabelle for not giving more warning that the man in question had followed her.

Turning, she looked into icy blue eyes and suddenly felt

the need to hide behind Stefan. Though the man matched Stefan in height as well as build, a cold bitter cynicism lay behind his eyes. Unruly black hair fell below his ears and when he smiled it reminded her of a gothic horror story where the man was really a werewolf.

"To what do we owe the honor, my lord?" Stefan asked in smooth tones.

"Why, Your Grace, you of all people should be privy to the reasons of my visit, that is unless—"

The man stopped with a cold gleam in his eye, flashing his teeth in a wickedly handsome smile and held up his hands. "My apologies, by the look on your face I can see you were not made aware of my visit. Very peculiar."

His voice was smooth with only a slight accent giving way to his foreign heritage. The new earl looked at Isabelle longer than Rosalind thought appropriate, his eyes intense and methodical, as they seemed to stroke across her ever curve, until Stefan cleared his throat.

"Apologies again, Your Grace. I do believe we will be seeing each other soon. Enjoy your evening, ladies." With a fluid bow he left. Rosalind gave an involuntary shiver before standing closer to Stefan.

"Well, he wasn't so bad." Isabelle finally broke the silence.

"Not so bad?" Rosalind wanted to shake her sister as she watched the man's disappearing form with more than curiosity. "Isabelle, listen to me. You are never to allow that man near you, do you understand?"

"Of course, Rose." Isabelle smiled and walked in the opposite direction away from her and Stefan.

"I feel a headache coming on." Rosalind said once alone with Stefan near the dancing.

He offered his arm and escorted her out of the crush. "Well, sweetheart, we only have to stay long enough to give the gossips something to talk about for tea during afternoon calls."

Rosalind clenched her teeth. The last thing she wanted was to be the object of gossip again. If anything it seemed the curse on their family wasn't death but to be perpetual gossip for the ton to sink their fangs into.

Leaning against Stefan as much as she could without thumbing her nose at propriety, she suddenly felt a tingling sensation in her legs. Her breathing slowed at a rapid rate. It was torture keeping her head up, if she just closed her eyes once, just one time.

"Rose," Stefan whispered near her head. "Rose?" His voice more urgent, she wanted to shake her head to tell him she was fine and that the spell would pass as it always did, instead she felt worse than previous times. If she could, she would be sucking in air faster than she currently was. Her lungs would not work, and her legs and arms were unable to move. Warm hands were suddenly on her, and she was lifted into the air as the black took over.

Stefan felt a sense of history repeating itself as Rosalind again fainted or fell asleep into his arms. Only this time, he was fortunate to be hidden away from the crush of people, which made it easier for him to escort her down the hall. Panic at her wellbeing overwhelmed the need he felt rush through his body at having her in his arms again. Clenching his teeth, he slowly made his way back towards the hallway near the far side of the room.

Finally reaching the darkened escape route, one arm held her while the other tried the doors. The first few were locked, finally nearing the end of the hallway and perspiring with the task at hand, the door finally gave. He rushed her in through the darkness, shuffling across the hard floor until his foot hit a stool.

Biting back an oath he continued towards the only light in the room, coming straight from the open curtains, the full moon.

The room was dead silent; he pulled Rosalind into his lap as he sat on the bench in the window.

"Rose?" He caressed her face, cursing his hands for shaking as they pushed back hair that had fallen across her cheekbone. God above, she was breathtaking. Her skin so soft that he could no more stop touching her than stop breathing. Her lips parted and let out a shallow breath of air.

Curious, he looked closer, tilted her towards the moonlight and noticed the shade of light blue across it.

This spell was not like the others.

"Propriety be damned," he said, turning her on his knee as he pulled at her dress, first unfastening the buttons with rapid speed, and then loosening her stays until he knew she could breathe. Once the dress was loose on her form he waited for color to return to her face. Cursing, he leaned in only to see the blue still across her lips.

What the devil was wrong with her?

He could do nothing save hold her and wait. Never had fear gripped his heart as strong as in that moment.

Finally, after an eternity, she stirred in his arms. "Rose!"

She coughed and moaned. Her eyes fluttered open and she tried to speak through pale lips.

"Rose?" He slowly patted her face, willing her eyes to open.

Her eyes fluttered open, like tiny pin points she kept opening and closing them as if trying to focus. "Stefan?"

"Yes, love. Careful. I, uh..." Blast. How was he to explain this predicament? *I unfastened your corset in your sleep?*

He groaned and changed the subject. "You couldn't

breathe. Do you remember anything?"

She choked on a sob and threw her arms around his neck. "It's never been like that before! I'm dying! Stefan, I know it. I should have told you. I hadn't a spell since the first ball we met at! I must be dying!"

He wasn't sure what alarmed him more, Rosalind unable to breathe or Rosalind giving into fear untypical of her normal strength.

"Love, look at me."

Shaking, she pulled back, he silently thanked God that her lips were returning to their cherry hue. "You are not dying."

"You don't know... I have these spells, and you don't know!"

"Rosalind, you are not dying. I won't allow it. And we've discussed this in detail. The spells were not affecting you when in the country side. There must be a simple explanation. I refuse to believe the curse has anything to do with it."

At that she laughed. "Oh, and how do you plan to stop my sleeping spells or my disease, Stefan? Merely order the angel of death to stay put?"

"If I have to." He chuckled. "Rose, other than your spells, you are a healthy, stubborn woman. We'll simply trust in that for now. And, I doubt your spells have been anything like this, have they?"

Slowly, she shook her head. "No, I've always been able to breathe. This time I felt as if the world was suffocating me. Everything was constricting and then my dress—"

She glanced down at the loose fabric and to Stefan's irritation it was at that exact moment that he heard someone try the door to the room.

Quickly, he pulled the curtains around them and lifted Rosalind further into the corner and onto his lap, the curtains easily covered them as long as the intruder didn't fancy a look at the moonlight.

He motioned for her to be still and quiet. She nodded, and if he wasn't so concerned about her health, his family, getting married, or the fact that something was causing everyone to die, he would be enjoying this moment. The smell of her skin trapped inside their alcove, her hair rubbing his chin and her supple body fitting snuggly into his, as if made for one another.

"Cheroot?" The voice sounded familiar, though it was hushed, as if the man was trying to disguise himself. Stefan couldn't quite pinpoint it, and he wasn't about to expose them by making a move to peek through the curtain.

"I did not travel all this way to share a smoke and brandy with you as you are well aware."

"Ah, yes, well. It was polite of me to ask, don't you think?" The man laughed nervously.

"Forgive me, but nothing about you seems polite." The other man said sternly. And then it hit Stefan, the one man was Dominique; his voice held that calculated smoothness. As if he needed to talk slow and concise lest his accent make a sudden appearance.

"You owe me," Dominique said plainly.

"It was a misunderstanding, my lord nothing more." The man coughed, his voice scratchy.

Dominique let out a beastly laugh. "A misunderstanding you say? How was it to be a misunderstanding when I discovered you tried to rob my own fortune away from me? Or are you referring to the misunderstanding when you set about murdering my valet?"

The room was dead silent.

"Or," Dominique chuckled. "Are you referring to the misunderstanding of blackmail, when you threatened to kill me once I exposed who fathered the youngest girl."

"That is quite enough, my lord!" The man yelled as best

he could with his voice still seemingly hoarse.

"Ah, a misunderstanding perhaps?" Dominique offered.

"Name your price."

"Money, as you well know, is no object. Yet I am wise enough to see that you have none to offer me, so it seems we are at an impasse, are we not?"

The man cursed. "I haven't any money, and you know it!"

"Ah, but what of value are you in possession of my good man? Therein lies the question. What are you willing to give that I do not already have?"

"Heartless beast! That's what you are!"

Dominique chuckled. "I've been called worse. Now, what are you willing to sacrifice for my silence at your indiscretions or as you put them misunderstandings?"

The silence in the room was deafening. Stefan could feel Rosalind's heart beating wildly in her chest.

Stefan wasn't sure how this would end, but it couldn't be good. Was not money the only currency in which men spoke?

"My daughter." The broke his silence. "If I give you my daughter, the youngest. Will that suffice?"

"That falls to you. How much would you say your daughter means to you?" Dominique asked.

"She's all I have, all I was allowed to have of her mother. When her mother married another… well, you can imagine." The man's voice trailed off.

"And if I accept. I will be the one making the terms of this contract, yes?"

"Yes." The man's voice was hoarse.

"Splendid. And considering it seems you are in desperate need of money. I shall strike a bargain with you."

"I'm listening." The man's voice perked up, sudden interest evident.

"You are to never visit her. Ever. When I take your

daughter, I will destroy her faith in men every day that I am with her. I will poison her against you. I will glory in your weakness as I expose to her the devil you really are. And if you die, she will not attend your funeral. I hope she laughs on that day, that the tears are from joy that her once beloved father is dead. If you can promise me all these rights, I will allot you the sum of one hundred thousand pounds."

"One hundred thousand pounds! That's a devil's fortune!"

"It seems your offer is too sweet for me to deny. Think of it as payment. You have sold your daughter to me. A gentleman's arrangement. Shall we shake on it?" Dominique asked his voice getting louder and sounding more irritated by the minute.

"Y-yes, my lord. When will you send for her?" the man asked.

Dominique let out a bark of laughter. "I assumed you understood. I will not be sending for her. I will be returning with her. Make the preparations. I shall send over the contract in the morning when my man picks her up."

"But!" the man yelled.

"A deal is a deal..." Dominique clipped.

The door clicked open and shut again.

The man was still lingering, and all Stefan could hear was weeping and words that were so horrible to his ears he couldn't bear it. "It will be worth it. It will all be worth it. My love, you will pay for your sins."

CHAPTER SEVENTEEN

Conscience doth make cowards of us all.
~ Hamlet ~

ROSALIND FELT STEFAN'S ARMS stiffen around her at the man's horrendous words. How could selling your own flesh and blood be worth anything but heartache? After the door clicked shut and they were sure both men had cleared the room, she slowly pushed away from Stefan.

"Did you recognize the voices?"

Stefan looked away. "Well, obviously one was Dominique, but the other... I wasn't able to decipher. Although I'll admit familiarity."

Rosalind bit her lip. "I kept thinking they would discover us, but they seemed..."

Stefan outwardly shuddered. "They seemed too intent on buying and selling, did they not?"

"We have to do something." Rosalind felt pity for the girl who was going to be sold into the man's dirty clutches! The same man who admitted no shame in abusing the woman he was to marry. She wasn't sure which was worse. The father knowingly selling his daughter for money or the man purchasing.

"Rose, as much as I would like to help. There is nothing we can do now. I'll try to find Dominique in the ball, if he's still here. Mayhap he'll listen to reason, if not, then… well we can at least try that much." He lifted her chin with his hand and brushed a kiss across her lips.

"Trust me?" he asked.

"Not that I was ever given a choice…" She smiled. "But yes, Stefan. I trust you."

"Can you manage?" His gaze traveled down her body marked with concern rather than passion.

"I'm fine, I assure you. Must have been another spell, like I said." With that she rose to her feet and let out a curse as her dress nearly fell to her ankles.

"Stefan!" Grabbing the material that was now cascading at a rapid pace, she covered herself as best as possible as her face heated. "I'm sure you were waiting until the appropriate time to tell me that my dress has magically come loose in my sleep?"

Stefan forced his hands into his pockets and cursed. "It was choking you! What would you have me do! Let you die!"

Biting back laughter, Rosalind looked at him. "So what you're saying is, by removing my dress, you've also saved my life, is that it, Your Grace?"

"Naturally." He shrugged, the devil's gleam in his eye as he tilted his head and looked at her form. "I believe I'm your savior, yet again."

"Are you now?" She lifted a brow.

"Absolutely. Don't saviors of damsels in distress normally receive… some sort of reward?"

With a wicked laugh, she fingered the loose corset strings, noting the hungry look in Stefan's eyes. Men, leave it to them to be distracted by a woman even in the face of danger. "A reward is what you seek?"

"'Tis only fair, my lady." Stefan's eye darkened as he closed the distance between them.

"And what type of woman would I be, if I was not fair, Your Grace?"

"My thoughts exactly," he murmured leaning down.

"Well then," Rosalind stepped back. "I'll be sure to reward you tomorrow. After all, we are being missed at the ball." Stefan's face was incredulous as his eyes flashed with unsated lust.

"Uh, that is to say... of course. I'll wait with baited breath." He kissed her hand and turned on his heel.

"Stefan?"

"Rosalind?"

"My dress, if you please." She turned her back and waited for his warm hands to torture her as he tightened her dress and set her to rights. He lifted her hair and made slow work of tightening her stays.

If the fires of Hades erupted in that very room, Rosalind would have merely shrugged — unfulfilled desire shot through her as Stefan slowly tightened her stays. Each tug sent a shiver down her arms and legs; would wicked behavior be so horrible? Her treacherous hands demanded she push down her dress and let him have his way with her.

But they were to be married so soon and although she knew him to be a good protector, he hadn't yet said the words she so desperately needed to hear. Love, it seemed, was never in the stars for Rosalind, but she could still hope that before she died he would utter those sacred words and just maybe look at her the way she so ached for.

"All done." His hands left her, causing an ache to stir in her heart.

"Lovely." She swallowed and managed to walk by the

giant man without falling prostrate, begging him to kiss her as he had before. Really, she felt quite fit for Bedlam at that moment. Her thoughts were just that, madness in its purest form.

There was nothing that could be done with her hair, to put it in the original arrangement would be near impossible. So she settled for a simple chignon and hoped nobody would notice it had changed. Exhaling, she reached for the door. Awareness of Stefan's nearness still trickled down her body. How was it that by just being near the man, she was ready to ask him to take her dress off again?

She has bewitched me. Stefan followed Rosalind's retreating form and swore He had nobody to confide in, not a single one. It seemed the only women he trusted enough to speak to just so happened to be the one that was driving him irrevocably insane. On cue, the object of his lust filled fantasy's turned towards the Dowager of Barlowe, making him instantly uncomfortable. The last thing he needed was for his grandmother to see him in his current state. Both women lifted a curious brow in his direction, and he suddenly felt like some recalcitrant schoolboy. Should he shuffle his feet and avert his eyes and add to the effect? Or approach the women in hopes that they were talking of the weather. Right, his grandmother talking of weather. He would laugh the day weather would replace gossip.

"Ladies," he said as he approached.

"Stefan my boy, why haven't you danced with the lady yet? She tells me she hasn't danced a single dance with her betrothed all evening! I expected more from my grandson." The Dowager continued to stare daggers through Stefan.

The air stole from his lungs when Rosalind bit her lip in

expectation of his question. "Would you care to dance?"

She took his gloved hand, and he led her to the middle of the dance floor. They hadn't danced together since the time in the meadow. Maybe it was the candlelight, or possibly inanity from the curse, but holding Rosalind in his arms felt special — right.

"So you can dance eloquently once indoors..." Rosalind turned in his arms. Devil take it, she felt good.

"Yes well, I prefer the snow and woodland creatures to the gossip of the ton any day."

"Don't forget Samson, though I imagine he was more jealous than entertained by our little dance."

Stefan quirked a smile at her mention of his horse. "You never told me what you were doing out dancing in the snow in the first place, nor the identity of your invisible dance partner, Rosalind."

She blushed to the roots of her hair. "I was dancing with a man from my dreams."

"Do you often dream of men?" He lifted a brow, suddenly interested in all of her mad fantasies, never mind that he wanted to kill any man real or made up that touched her, including the married ones.

As he pulled her closer, his hands glided down the curve of her dress. He had never discovered a more perfect fit for his hand, and in that moment wondered if there ever would be anything that belonged so rightfully in his arms.

Rosalind cleared her throat. "I don't often dream of men. Just one."

"One? So he's real? Where is he? I'll destroy him! You are mine, Rosalind. Never forget who you belong to. It is I who crave the taste of your lips. I who desire you in my bed from now until forever... and it is I who will slay your dragons and storm the castle to win your love." His grip tightened as he pulled her body as close as he could during the dance. "And it is I who will make slow agonizing love to you until your body is sated..." The dance ended, he had yet to release her. "Nobody else..." His voice was gruff filled with lust, grief, and jealousy. Why the devil was he shaking?

"Stefan?" Rosalind lifted a gloved hand to his face.

"Yes?" He swallowed the lump in his throat.

"It *is* you."

Her warm hand abandoned his face. Rosalind left him wanting, needing, gasping for air and feeling lost all at the same time. Whatever did she mean? The time spent thinking on her cryptic words was interrupted when Gwen nearly ran into him.

"She's gone."

How was it that he was cursed with so many females in his life? Did they always talk in riddles? "Yes, well, I'm sure we'll find her." He patted her shoulder. The poor thing was probably exhausted after being at her first ball.

"No, Your Grace. It's Isabelle. She's gone! I know she wouldn't leave the ball without us. I just know it! Something dreadful has happened!"

"Stay calm, I'm sure we'll find her." Stefan threw her a charming smile and walked off in search of Rosalind, taking his time making greetings with other attendees the entire way.

Later that night, they figured Isabelle had gone missing around the same time Rosalind and Stefan had gone into the library.

The last place they needed to look was the house in town. For where else would Isabelle had run off to?

As Stefan pounded on the door and his grip tightened on Rosalind. The valet opened, his expression grave.

"She's gone" Willard announced.

"It seems to be the general consensus." Stefan muttered pushing past him. "Now tell me, do you have any idea where she's run off to?"

"I've made arrangements." Lady Hariss made her way down the stairs. "I'm afraid there's nothing that can be done now."

"You've made arrangements for what exactly?" Stefan asked his stomach feeling tight with dread.

The dowager gave a mad smile and fanned herself with her naked hand. "Oh, well, you two were just taking such a dreadfully long time getting married. We needed money; you gave me no other option. The contract has been signed. Now, if you'll excuse me. I'm tired."

"What the devil are you talking about?" Stefan tried to keep himself calm as the wicked woman gave out a menacing laugh.

"She was a bastard anyway, it's of no matter."

With that she marched up the stairs.

Stefan could hear the two sisters weeping next to him. Was he the only one confused?

CHAPTER EIGHTEEN

They do not love that do not show their love
~ The Two Gentleman of Verona ~

ROSALIND WATCHED HER MOTHER'S disappearing form and fought the urge to throw something at her. Was madness then her mother's curse?

She turned to the Willard, who now appeared to be sweating and ready to kill anything that spoke to him. "Do you know what she speaks of? Where Isabelle ran off to? Why she claims that the youngest is a bastard?"

He cleared his throat. "Surely, you don't think I had anything to do with this? Your mother is ill my lady, it would be good of you to remember that. If your mother felt the need to sell her youngest daughter to the highest bidder, then so be it. After all, is it so odd for a peer to betroth a daughter in order to gain an alliance as well as money?" He lifted a haughty eyebrow and turned on his heel, muttering under his breath.

"But..." Rosalind wanted to remind him that her mother

had no reason for her claim, but felt Stefan's hands on her shoulders. The pressure of his hands made her relax, best not to ask the valet any information at this point. The look in his eyes was pure rage and madness.

She watched helplessly as the man walked away, leaving her alone with Gwen and Stefan.

"Stefan," Rosalind's voice hitched. "What do we do? Everything has gone topsy-turvy…"

Stefan didn't move for a while, his muscular form rigid. "We must marry immediately."

"Oh sweet heavens, here we go again." Rosalind rubbed her forehead with her hands. "Have you learned nothing about proposals, Stefan? Besides, we already agreed to marry."

"He's right, m'lady." Mary said behind her.

"Oh, Mary, I didn't see you! Have you seen Isabelle?"

Mary's posture was slumped as if she carried the weight of the world on her shoulders. "I'm afraid she's gone."

"But where!" Rosalind was tired of fighting, tears streamed down her face. How had everything gone so horribly wrong? Stefan was back to his insulting proposals, her sister was missing, her mother insane.

"There's nothing we can do for her now." Mary handed a piece of parchment to Stefan and walked away, eyes downcast. Her nurse and godmother had been missing these past few days, or at least scarce around the house. Possibly, madness was catching up with everyone. Was there any other explanation?

Rosalind watched as Stefan unfolded the paper and read the contents, his face turning redder with rage by the minute.

"Off to bed, all of you," he barked.

Rosalind bit back a curse, wanting nothing more than to yell and scream at him. How dare he yell when she was so distraught!

She opened her mouth to speak. His large hand came slicing through the air in front of her making her stop from saying something she would most likely regret.

"To bed, both of you." The warmth in Stefan's eyes faded and Rosalind was once again reminded of the brute behind the man she had grown to care for.

Nodding mutely, she turned on her heel and marched to bed, holding Gwen's hand the entire way up the treacherous staircase.

The last word she heard from Stefan's mouth as she turned the corner to go down the hall was, "Dominique."

CHAPTER NINETEEN

For truth is always strange, stranger than fiction.
~ Lord Byron ~

STEFAN PACED THE ENTRYWAY for what seemed like hours. Finally, he went into the study and poured himself a brandy, still looking at the letter as if it would somehow grow lips and begin speaking to him. Perhaps he better put down the brandy before he imagined more enchantments in the house. Next thing he would think his horse was talking to him. On second thought...

"Rubbish, that's complete rubbish." Stefan shook the thought from his head. Was it a possibility that all of them were to go mad until the marriage was done?

The truth, in black and white ink, lay before him. But more than that, was a clue he hadn't been expecting.

It was a contract signed by Dominique, the new earl, to purchase the youngest daughter... but if this was the same daughter the man was talking about in the library at the ball that meant either Rosalind's father wasn't dead, or he wasn't the rightful father to Isabelle. The more likely story.

So who was her father? And why would the contract be sent here? He looked down again and noticed the scratchy handwriting of the Dowager Countess of Hariss. Next to her name was the family crest.

He couldn't very well run after Isabelle. Her own family had legally sold her to the new earl in a betrothal contract. A sum of a hundred thousand pounds in exchange for one tiny girl.

Closing his eyes against the torment of emotions, he sent up a brief prayer for Isabelle's safety, and glanced back down at the script.

On the bottom edge of the paper was a tiny riddle. Why it would be on the contract in the first place was beyond him. The fact that it was there was nothing more than an answered prayer. He studied it until his eyes felt like they were sand.

Sometime during the night, it fell from his fingers as he dozed off to sleep.

Rosalind went in search of Stefan first thing in the morning. Her goal was to give him a piece of her mind as to how proposals were to work and to also convince the duke to go in search of her sister. After all, she couldn't be far.

She found him snoring in her father's old study. Not that it was a huge revelation to see him snoring with his mouth open, but it made her smile nonetheless. With a smile, she slammed the door shut earning a curse from the sleeping man and a very amusing debacle as he righted himself from falling out of his chair.

"Oh, my apologies, did I wake you?" She sang as she walked to the curtains and threw them open, allowing light to stream in. Stefan was sitting, eyes blazing with a piece of paper in hand and an empty bottle of brandy next to him.

"Long night?" She took a seat next to him and noted he looked quite put out, as if he was ready to strangle her for speaking in his presence, that should teach him to get so deep into his cups or continue to propose to her as if she were nothing more than a statue.

"Yes." His eyes closed as he leaned back against the chair. "Of course I was having this lovely dream of a beautiful redhead until some witch slammed the door and let in so much sunlight that I find myself ready to curse any sort of sunny weather."

The sun chose that particular moment to blaze into his eyes making his arms flap at his face like a bird trying to fly away from the inevitable heat.

"Son of a—"

"—Stefan!"

"Apologies... It was a long night. To say the least. My intention wasn't to drown my sorrows in whiskey, nor was it to fall asleep at this particular angle that-thanks to the uncomfortable seat will leave the most lovely crick in my neck come later this afternoon."

Rosalind swallowed, slowly taking in Stefan's mood and went to ring for tea before taking her seat. "Did you find anything of use?"

"How are you at riddles, love?"

"Riddles? Hmm, well I'd like to believe I've figured you out, so that makes me what? A relative genius?"

"Ah a sense of humor in the morning. How positively irritating," Stefan muttered as he thrust the paper in front of her face. "If you can figure this out, I just may eat my horse."

Rosalind grinned. "Poor Samson. I wonder how he'd feel to know he was part of such a wager."

"I can assure you, Rose, that Samson is mindlessly trotting around the estate eating oats out of the hands of each stable hand as we speak. He won't think a thing of it. I swear he's gained two stone since we've been here."

Taking the paper from his outstretched hand, Rosalind let out a little laugh despite Stefan's sour mood and began reading. It appeared to be a normal betrothal contract. Her mother's signature with the signet ring of her late father on the side.

She shrugged. "Sorry to say, but it looks completely normal..." With a huff she brought the parchment closer to her face noticing a small etching on the bottom part of the paper. "Except..."

"Yes," Stefan rose from his chair and stretched. "Except for that blasted riddle on the bottom of the page. Unfortunately I took French at university instead of Russian, terrible language if you ask me, but it seems we are in need of a translator."

"Gwen."

"Of course, the other sister why hadn't I thought of that?" Stefan looked around in exasperation. The night had obviously not been kind to him, she had half a mind to put him outside with Samson until his barbaric manners were all but gone. Who knew he was such a bear in the morning! If anyone had something to be upset about it was her!

"No," Rosalind scowled at Stefan at the same time the sunlight again enhanced his god-like body. On second thought, she walked to him and wrapped her arms tight around his neck in excitement. "But she knows Russian."

"Do I want to know how she knows?" His body relaxed the minute it was in contact with hers. Shuddering, he bent down to kiss her forehead.

"She knows several languages; it's a type of hobby for her. I'll go search for her while you go... do what men do to get ready in the morning and do try not to be grouchy."

"If you don't want me to be grouchy then you need to

marry me."

"Now?" she asked sarcastically.

He was obviously not amused, for he cursed and ran both hands through his long blond hair.

"Yes, right now. Immediately."

"Are you still drunk?"

"I am not!" Stefan closed his eyes. "I am not drunk. I just think it best for us to be married. I can provide protection for you and your sisters."

Not the most romantic proposal and most definitely not the words that she wanted to hear from his lips, but his reason was sound.

Her shoulder slumped and she nodded. "Tonight, we'll marry tonight. Does that suit you?"

With a grin so magnetic that Rosalind couldn't help but smile back, he laughed and nodded. "Oh it suits me just fine. Now, go find your sister while I make preparations."

With a nod, she was out the door in search for Gwen, praying the entire way that she still remembered Russian.

CHAPTER TWENTY

It is useless to tell one not to reason but to believe —
You might as well tell a man not to wake but sleep.
~ Lord Byron ~

BY THE TIME STEFAN returned to his townhome, he knew his family had indeed gone mad. Fitz was worsening, looking as if he was on his death bed. His mother was bed ridden with orders to rest, and Elaina and James were running around the house as if the dratted sky was falling.

"Stefan!" Elaina ran into his arms the minute he opened the door. Her chocolate eyes were dim compared to their usual shine. How he had ever found her attractive especially now that he had Rosalind in his life, he would never know.

Prying her hands away from his body, he asked her the question he didn't want to ask. "Is Fitz alive?"

"Of course he's alive! Everyone's alive! It's the matter of impending death that has the servants and everyone within this house mad! And you've done nothing!"

The things he wanted to say to her were grossly

inappropriate, and he knew she spoke only out of fear. "I'm to marry this evening."

"It will do nothing." She slumped onto the stairway and put her head in her hands. "Believe me, this curse will be the ruin of us all."

Not that he was known for being an emotional man, but this really wasn't the time for comforting anyone, so he stepped over her as best he could and readied himself for his upcoming nuptials. Knowing that if this didn't work, there was something else a foot, and he was going to figure it out even if it did kill him.

It was a wonder what fresh clothes did for his outlook on the depressing day. Remembering Rosalind's words, he tried to paste a smile on his face instead of a scowl, but it was blasted hard, all things considered.

Samson waited for him outside the house — the horse truly had gained weight since their little endeavor back into London.

"So what do you think Samson? Today we are to be married. No more bachelorhood."

Was it him or did Samson slump his shoulders as if disappointed? No, it had to be his vivid imagination; it seemed in the past week he had done nothing except imagine that the world around him was enchanted and alive.

"Blasted curse has me going mad," he mumbled, getting on his horse. As he turned the corner he noticed the valet walking hastily towards his residence.

"Good day, Your Grace." Mr. Fitzgerald gave a curt bow and meant to be on his way. Samson however was not having any of it. He neighed and kicked until Stefan was sure the horse would trample the small man.

"Samson! Down this instant! Heel!" Stefan pulled tighter on the reigns. Was madness also taking over his horse?

Finally, the horse calmed down and promptly sneezed in

the valet's face. Making Stefan cough to cover his laugh. What had gotten into him?

"Apologies, I don't believe I've ever seen him react this way. Must be the curse." Stefan offered a small laugh, but the valet was not amused.

"Good day." Mr. Fitzgerald tipped his hat and walked off.

Stefan turned Samson back down the street. "Don't know if I should congratulate you or strangle you for sneezing on a man. Whatever has gotten into you, old boy?"

Samson's only response was to huff and continue trotting on.

Gwen looked again at the tiny scribbles and sighed. "I'm sorry Rose, I just can't make out what it's saying. I believe it may actually be in German, not Russian as you assumed, and by the markings, it seems to not be a riddle but some sort of directions. The only thing I can make out is the words *beware the Black Forest*."

Rosalind mumbled an oath. They had been sitting and discussing what to do of the past two hours, and neither of them had any inclination as to what the cryptic words meant!

It didn't help that Rosalind's mind was thick with worry for her sister and selfishly, for her upcoming wedding that night. Hadn't she always sworn she wouldn't marry a man based off of the stupid curse? And here she was doing that very thing. Sure, her heart was involved she possibly even loved Stefan, but did he love her? Or was he merely offering his protection and his bed?

Gwen was still talking, "Rose, did you hear what I said?"

"Hmm? What? I'm sorry, woolgathering, I guess."

With an exhale Gwen folded the paper and put it on her

dresser. "Rose, I miss her too. I don't know if mother's merely mad or if we truly are cursed, but let us try to be happy. After tonight everything should be over with. The curse and the madness with it, and then mother will be able to tell us about her whereabouts."

Rosalind looked at her sister's porcelain face. Such a beautiful girl. "I'll try, for your sake, I'll try. Shall we begin to ready ourselves for tonight?"

"Yes." Gwen kissed Rose on the forehead and moved to close the door.

"What were you discussing?" their mother asked, barging into the room. "If you mean to go after your sister, you'll never find her. I ask that you trust my judgment in this. She is in good hands. After all..." She walked to the window and began moving back and forth as if in a trance. "I am a mother. It is my job to see all my girls married off. Isn't that right Rose? And see how much you've pleased me today? The curse will be broken. I will no longer be ill, and you'll be a duchess. Yes, yes, it has worked out perfectly." She wrung her hands together until Rosalind's own hands began to hurt. "I imagine everything will be perfect by morning." She turned around to face them, her face haggard and worn. "Yes, by morning everything will return to normal, my loves, and Edward, yes he will be back too. He loves me you know."

"Mother," Rosalind took a tentative step towards the dowager. "Father's dead, remember?" Never mind that his name was not Edward, but possibly her mother was just confused.

"Oh yes, yes, he is, isn't he?" She clapped her hands together as if excited by the idea. "Now, we must ready you for your wedding! Yes, we must get ready for the ceremony." With a gleeful laugh, she left.

Gwen and Rose shared a look of pure horror before Rosalind rushed to the door and locked it.

"She's mad!" Rosalind lifted a shaking hand to her temple.

"She is..." Gwen licked her lips. "And I'd die before I'd let her ruin this for you Rose, I swear it." Her sister walked over to ring for her maid.

"What are you doing?"

"I'm calling for the valet. He has some sort of tea that he's been giving mother to subdue her. I'm going to ask him to double the dosage."

"Is it dangerous?" Rosalind asked putting her hand over her sisters.

Gwen shrugged. "He says it's a mild sedative. Mother and father used to put it in our tea when we were young to help us sleep. I'm sure it will be fine."

Rosalind nodded, but in the back of her mind a memory flared to life. The tea she was forced to drink every night when she was young and how her body would feel sluggish in the morning. She had stopped for a few years until her first debut into society when she had trouble sleeping again; her mother began putting it in her tea saying it would ease her nerves.

The maid entered, and Gwen gave instructions, but Rosalind's mind continued to wander.

"Shall we begin with your hair?" Gwen asked reaching her hands into the silky locks flowing down Rosalind's back.

Rosalind looked at her reflection in the mirror and fought the urge to cry. What was the matter with her? In all her haste, she had agreed to marry a man who botched every marriage proposal given, and to be quite frank he had been given many chances to be romantic. Did he love her? Was it merely to break the curse? Or get her in bed?

If she was to be introspective about her own feelings she would admit that yes, she was marrying to break the curse. It had to be. Perhaps if they had more time, to court, and to woo as she has originally asked, but now it seemed they were out of time, if her mother's strange murmurings were any indication.

Tonight she would be the Duchess of Montmouth. Why, she wondered as Gwen began brushing her hair, did it leave her sick in the stomach?

"Ready?" Stefan asked as his hand reached for Rosalind's.

Her heart thumped in her chest, she was shaking so much she was sure Stefan could feel the nervousness. "Ready."

Both turned towards the front of the small church where only their respective families lay in wait.

Forgoing tradition, Stefan had wanted to hold Rosalind's hand as he walked her down the aisle, for she hadn't a father to escort her, and he had no father to offer her. It was as if two sad orphans made their way to the final destiny laid out before them.

He squeezed her hand and stole a glance at her beautifully adorned dress. In that moment, Stefan hated himself, for in the end he took full blame for the deaths of their families and the weight settled over his shoulders as he watched his soon to be wife, shaking next to him. Rosalind, the woman was perfect, untouchable, pure, and she above all women deserved to be worshipped by the ton, deserved to have her father kiss her hand and demand that Stefan be a good husband.

I swear it, Stefan thought to himself as they reached the front of the church. *I swear on my life that I will make you proud, deceased parents of ours. That your blood line will be strong, that I will spend every waking moment of my life making hers better, and every dream filled sleep holding her in my arms.*

The ceremony was short and to the point. The vows were read, and Rosalind wore a sad smile as she looked to her mother, who still looked as mad as ever. The church was near empty, and Stefan felt indignation rise in his chest, along with failure. And Stefan cursed the curse, if that were possible, all over again. She deserved flowers, a woman with such red hair and beautiful nature — well it wasn't right that she didn't have the wedding she deserved surrounded by all her sisters, friends, family...

Stefan shook the thought away. No sense worrying over what he could not fix, then again he did have a surprise in store for her tonight. Yes, tonight had been hard for him to arrange considering both of their houses were filled with the mad and sick because of the curse.

Like a nervous school-boy, he helped Rosalind into the carriage. It came to his large home but instead of stopping up front, it went around to the back of the house.

"Where are we going? The servants' entrance?" Rosalind winked and Stefan nearly lost his nerve.

"You'll see." He patted her hand and watched in fascination as his bride's eyes took in the scene around him. Daylight had given way to twilight. The sky was starting to scatter with stars, and he could not help but smile to himself. He wasn't the most romantic man in the world, and he knew Rosalind's only view of him was a barbaric, but he wasn't the selfish sort of lover that most men were. No, he wanted to take his time with Rosalind. If he failed to woo her during their courtship, he would damn well woo her during their lovemaking, until she was marked as his.

The carriage pulled to a stop, he could have sworn his hands were sweating in his gloves as he held out his hand for Rosalind. With a curious smile, she followed him through the back of the property.

"A cottage?" Rosalind's eyes widened, and selfishly he

hoped it was in pure shock at the expanse of décor.

The cottage was covered in snow, but the trail leading up was scattered with red rose petals.

"For my Briar Rose, the fairest of the fair..." he whispered in her ear. "Shall we?"

Rosalind's laughter echoed off the enchanted path, "Briar Rose hmm? Am I then a thorn within the rose?"

Stefan stopped in his tracks and pulled her body flush against his. "No, my duchess. I would gladly prick my finger on your thorn if the result would be merely to gaze upon your face for the remainder of my days."

Her eyes pooled with unshed tears, but she turned and followed the rose drizzled path until they reached the door, not once responding to his speech.

"It's beautiful." Tears freely fell down Rosalind's porcelain skin as her eyes settled on the open door. A roaring fire and a picnic of fairy cakes lay in wait on the table. The massive bed in the middle of the room had its fair share of rose petals. The smell was intoxicating. Stefan had said to spare no expense when he gave instructions to Rosalind's mother. A moment of weakness or a moment of kindness — he wasn't certain which, but her mother had asked if she could prepare something special for the couple, and he had allowed it. On one condition. She must do it on his terms.

He wanted it to be perfect. And it was.

"Rose?"

Turning towards him, the new duchess smiled, igniting the passion Stefan had been carefully keeping at bay for the past few days. "I was wrong."

Stefan laughed, unable to help the jolly sound resounding from his belly. "Oh, those words sound so beautiful from your lips m'dear. Care to explain?" His hands fell to her soft skin on their own accord as he brought her lips closer to his own.

Rosalind leaned in and kissed him lightly on the mouth.

Oh madness, take him now! He was so on fire for her; surely his body would burn up before he was able to take her the way he wanted.

"You," she said again drawing his attention back to conversation. "Are able to be romantic."

"Yes well," Stefan stuttered unable to focus on anything but her lips. "I did write a sonnet just in case the roses didn't work."

"Oh, did you now?" Rosalind laughed.

"Yes, and I must admit I had Samson waiting in the back tied to a tree in case you needed more convincing. He can, at times, be very persuasive."

"Not unlike his master." Rosalind's eyes glanced at his lips and back into his eyes.

"Not at all like his master, Rosalind. Not at all..." His lips crushed hers forcefully and with a hunger he'd never experienced until that night. With a growl, he had her in his arms pressed against the same door they had just entered.

CHAPTER TWENTY-ONE

Love will find a way through paths where wolves fear to prey.
~ Lord Byron ~

ROSALIND COULDN'T REMEMBER A time when she had felt so many emotions at once. As Stefan's body pressed tighter against her, his arousal and passion evident. She could do nothing to stop the surge of joy that escaped her lips, nor the brazen ideas her body had.

Her mind told her she was doing this for the curse, that she merely needed to consummate the marriage and be done with the whole ordeal.

Her heart, however, was having a hard time believing that sound logic. It cried out for Stefan's heart and soul in a way more dangerous than she ever thought possible. For she knew the moment this fairy tale was over, the ending would be nothing but heartache. For every happy ending in existence spoke of love — *not* curses.

Soft yet powerful lips nibbled her neck. Strong masculine hands tangled in her hair. Dizzy with excitement, she didn't even realize Stefan had stopped kissing her until the warmth of his body left her.

Opening her eyes, she scanned the room. He was on the other side pouring a glass of wine.

"I promised I would woo you, and I will if it nearly kills me." Stefan said.

"But," Rosalind looked around the room. "We're already married, the wooing is done." She fought to keep her mind from focusing on such a tragic thought.

With a laugh, Stefan brought the cup to his lips, but did not drink, instead he placed his goblet next to the bed. "I have much to teach you, my dear. For the wooing has just begun. I pity the man that believes a courtship must die with marriage."

Chills ran up and down Rosalind's body as her shaky hand reached out to grab the wine he held out for her. "So tonight…" She couldn't finish the sentence.

"Tonight…" Stefan raised his glass in a toast. "Is just the beginning."

Forgoing her wine, Rosalind reached out and skimmed her fingers lightly over Stefan's broad chest. A low groan rumbled in his throat as he hastily threw the wine glass to the floor, shattering it before his arms reached out and grabbed Rosalind by the elbows, pulling her into his frame. Trapped by his embrace, Rosalind was unable to move away as he closed his eyes.

His breath fanned across her lips as he leaned down and merely breathed in her scent. Allowed his lips to roam down her neck, no kissing, no nibbling, almost as if he wanted his mouth to memorize the way her skin felt merely pressed against them.

Stefan's warm hands slowly moved from her elbows up to her shoulders and slowly, delicately pulled down the loose sleeved dress, causing her shoulders to be bare. A chill ran up and down her spine as she watched in fascination as Stefan's hands continued their torturous exploration and caress of her smooth skin. The temptation to moan was so extreme, she didn't know if she could stay silent. Yet, the man was only touching her. Nothing more; nothing less. The very thought that he had so much control and power over her left her feeling vulnerable. Deciding to take things into her own hands, she smoothly put her hands across his and slid them up his arms noticing his muscles flex beneath the curve of her fingers. Fear numbed her fingers making it difficult for her to do much else but touch him.

His wicked smile widened. "What are you doing?"

Voice trembling, she answered, "You've been teaching me lessons, have you not? What kind of student would I be if I didn't learn from my teacher? I'm merely mirroring your actions." Her hands moved to his jacket, but they betrayed her, shaking as she helped him out of it, softly pressing her palm to his chest feeling the warmth through his shirtsleeves and trying with all her might not to tremble with desire as his eyes turned black. His teasing gaze was all but gone, and in its place something far fiercer. Fear fought with excitement as Stefan grabbed her hands and thrust them above her head, tumbling her onto the bed with little effort. His hands still held hers. Breathing ragged, she noticed how her breath seemed to come out in shorts gasps as he gazed upon her face then lower and lower until she knew she had to be bright red. Never had she been more nervous. Not knowing what to say, she merely stared at his muscular form as he hovered over her.

"Tonight, I am still the teacher, and you, my sweet Rose, will be the pupil. Have you any complaints with that?"

Rosalind shook her head as Stefan's head closed in around hers, his lips caressing hers as he spoke.

"Good, because I have a lot to teach you and apparently a lot to prove. After all, my sonnets are stupid, my manners horrendous, my proposals ridiculous, and my romance in dire need of improvement. It appears I have only this one night, this one chance to prove to you that I can truly be the prince who rescues the princess. The one to make you scream out with pleasure — first seeking yours then my own... yes, this will be the night that you, my beauty, will sleep a deep sleep of satisfaction, for I lay myself — all of me — at your very feet."

Would it be terribly rude for her to tell him to stop talking? For at that moment she was ready for anything he wanted to give to her. And his talking, his romancing, was driving her mad. Possession and desire overwhelmed her.

Moved to tears, Rosalind closed her eyes. If she could not see him, then perhaps her heart would not become more engaged. And then he kissed her, very softly across her lips. A more reverent kiss she had never experienced, for it spoke of promises, of love, and devotion. It was the way she had always wanted to be kissed, and when she opened her eyes, a single tear fell. For Stefan, the brute of a duke was looking at her the way she had always wanted to be looked at.

With adoration. So instead of closing her eyes again, or fighting his onslaught of passion. She lifted, very slightly, her head towards his and returned his soft kiss, allowing her tongue to run across his bottom lip. Scared out of her wits, she finally decided, she would give him all — everything she had — and hope it would be enough.

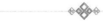

Stefan watched the torment of emotions play across Rosalind's face. A decision had been made, and he could tell the very second it happened. For Rosalind arched, reached towards him and kissed him. A more innocent and beautiful kiss Stefan had never encountered. Her velvet tongue ran across his lips and then slowly, agonizingly she opened her mouth to him. Everything seemed new and alive. The smell of roses drifted around him dancing across the room. The fire roared and spat in the distance, the snow fell lightly across the ground when he glanced out the window. And his wife, his beautiful treasure, was irresistible. Her large green eyes and soft porcelain skin caused him to ache to touch her forever, to never let his hands leave her body. He would never get tired of the way her silky skin felt beneath his rough hands. Or the way her hair appeared to be on fire.

He reached out and grabbed handful of hair thrusting his hands deeper into the mass of red perfection and let out a groan as he lifted it and at the same time lifted Rosalind to a sitting position on the bed. With little effort, he had her leaning against the large wooden bed. Like a perfect doll, she sat. With a mischievous grin, that he couldn't have helped even if he wanted to, he stripped himself of his shirt. Rosalind's eyes widened. A smile quirked at her lips. The minx, he had forgotten she had already seen him in all his glory. And now he wondered, would the thrill still be present?

Her hand reached out and caressed his muscled stomach. He let out a short gasp as her nails dug into his flesh as she reached around and pulled him down to her.

"Has the lesson then commenced?"

With a smug grin, he shook his head. "Not even close, my love, not even close."

Laughing, he pulled at her dress. Scandalized, she was not. With a joint effort, he stripped her until all that was left was her corset and chemise. He could see the outline of her body through the moonlight and firelight. And wondered if a man could truly die when he gazed upon such beauty. Soft curves framed her tall form and he found his mouth run completely dry as his eyes took in the glorious picture in front of him.

"Stefan?" she asked, slightly covering herself. Cursing himself for openly gawking at her, he made quick work of her corset, all the while hoping she wouldn't lose her nerve, not now.

"You are—" he said untying the first of her several laces "—by far—" another was loosened "—the most tantalizing woman I have ever seen."

She let out a gasp as he roughly pulled another lace. Fingers numbly went about loosening the rest of her laces. For a half moment, he wondered if Rosalind would be terribly upset if he decided upon cutting up her corset rather than unlacing her. Surely he could have saved time.

As his brain was getting used to the idea, he noticed a shiver run through Rosalind. It was quick, her head was bowed, and the thought hit him. Could she possibly be afraid? Perhaps fearful of him? Laying a hand on her shoulder, he allowed his other hand to untie the last of the laces. A rapid heartbeat pulsed through the heat of his hand.

Feeling slightly guilty for being so rough with her before, and tossing her on the bed like some Cyprian, Stefan took a deep breath and braced her shoulders, turning her towards him as her corset slipped to the floor, leaving the beauty in nothing save her chemise and silk stockings.

As he gazed upon the woman who had so captured his heart, he realized he must truly humble himself before her. Not in a proposal, not even because he was trying to be romantic, but because his heart demanded he give fully to her what was hers.

So, on his knees he went, taking a bow as he pressed a kiss to her palm and then her wrist. At a slow pace, Stefan took hold of the chemise and lifted it higher and higher until his eyes rested on the most beautiful expanse of creamy white leg, he had ever seen in his existence. Bestowing a kiss upon her thigh, he continued to lift, until he was face to face with his wife and the chemise was tossed away from her body.

A war raged within Rosalind's eyes. Any virgin would want to cover herself up, turn red, or possibly scream, but Rosalind's eyes never left his as she boldly stood before him, offering him everything.

He seized her hand and brought it to his lips, all the while leading her slowly back to the bed and laying her down before him. Tension radiated through her body as he reached for her stockings and with a smile pulled both off and threw them in the general direction of the discarded clothes.

One kiss, two kisses, three kisses up her leg until he reached the curve of her hips. Four kisses, five, and then six, it took him to arrive at her delicate shoulder. Seven kisses, eight, and finally nine as he bestowed a kiss across her lips, he knew being in Rosalind's arms was where he belonged.

His mouth slanted possessively across hers. Opening to him, she deepened the kiss, equaling his fervor and wrapped her arms around his neck drawing him closer into her warmth.

Desire exploded through him as her hands swirled across his back. She clung to his chest whimpering as she bit his bottom lip, holding it captive between her teeth.

Stefan plunged his tongue again into her mouth. His desire to taste her was so strong he thought to never stop kissing her. With a moan, he seized her body and rolled across the bed, allowing her to lie across him for just an instant, as he wanted to see the outline of her curves through the firelight.

Apparently, going slow was going to prove more difficult than he once thought. Stefan tried to focus on anything but the blood roaring through his ears as Rosalind's hands began to smoothly explore his body.

"Enough," he said gruffly, grabbing her hands, and turning her on her back yet again. "Enough." He hesitated a second before stripping the remainder of his clothes and joined her yet again, skin on skin, heat radiating from their bodies. He swore no other man would ever touch her, would ever know her. The last thoughts he had before making her his wife.

Rosalind awoke with a smile on her face. Slightly embarrassed at her behavior the night before, she was surprised she felt as rested as she did, especially considering her husband had her up half the night with his lovemaking, a fact Rosalind was not at all ashamed of.

Thirsty, she looked to the right of the bed and noticed her wine glass. Trying not to wake Stefan, she reached for the glass just as his arm came crashing around her body.

"Are you well, Rose?" His voice was haggard with sleep.

"More than well, Stefan. I was merely thirsty."

He sat up in the bed and rubbed her back, massaging the tight muscles as she lifted the cup to her lips.

Rosalind drank the contents of her wine, relishing the taste of sweet berries, and… what was that other unfamiliar taste? In question she raised her eyes to Stefan's ready to speak, but the words would not come.

Shaking her head against the dizziness she saw in front of her, she tried again, but her lips would not move, her body it seemed was paralyzed. This was no sleeping spell. This was, something much worse.

"Rose? *Rose!*" Stefan was shaking her body, the last thing she saw through the blurry haze of nothingness was a lone tear run down Stefan's cheek. And then blackness.

"Rose!" Stefan's body seemed frozen in place. How could he help her? He looked down at her lips, red as a Rose, yet paralyzed, her eyes now closed. The wine, it had to be the wine.

Cursing he leaned down to listen to her heart, it still beat. She was alive, yet he didn't know how long or what would happen if he didn't get the poison out of her system.

A menacing laughter pierced through the night sky.

"Finally! Do you think it was easy spying on the two of you? Lying in wait until you drank of the wine? I thought I would go mad at the sound of your wicked lovemaking. Is she gone then?" The Dowager Countess of Hariss burst through the door, dagger in hand. "He told me how much to use, and I believe I got it just right. Not truly enough to kill her, but I dare say it would take a miracle for her to wake up. Don't you think?" The dowager's eyes were blazing with hate.

"Your own daughter!" Stefan's scream was hoarse. "How could you do this to your own family!"

"Your family has taken everything that I've loved, Your Grace. I believe we're even."

It took everything in Stefan not to charge the mother and drive the dagger straight through her heart. "I've done nothing! The curse has made you mad!"

With a scream, she kicked the table over and began pulling at her own hair. "You have done everything! You and your wretched family! If I didn't have to marry into your family, I could have been happy."

She took a seat on the bed, her fingers slowly grazing the edge of the dagger, back and forth back and forth. Laughing, she looked up at Stefan again. "I was to be married before I met Rosalind's father. Of course you didn't know that, but your grandfather did. Because of the curse, I was forced to marry. Imagine everyone's surprise when I could not gain children from my husband? They blamed me, they all blamed me!"

A tear escaped down her cheek. Stefan realized the only

thing he could do was merely sit and wait for the woman to calm down before he stripped her weapon and tied her up. He draped a blanket over Rosalind, and waited for the woman to continue her insane speech, all the while trying to keep a trained eye on Rosalind in hopes that she wasn't worsening by the minute.

"Blamed you?" Stefan managed to sound curious. "For what?"

"They said my wickedness caused my husband harm! They said—" she panted for breath "—that if I didn't give him children, the curse would take over the families. It wasn't enough that we married. We needed children..."

"You have children. You sold one and are attempting to kill another..." Probably not the best time to remind the woman of her madness, but Stefan's anger was having a hard time staying at bay. A whimper escaped Rosalind. At least she was making noise. Panic seized his heart. He could not lose her now. He couldn't live if he did.

"They are not my children!" She wailed. "None of them! Edward is their father."

"Are you not their mother?" Stefan noticed Rosalind's eyes flutter. Thank you, God, he thought.

"I carried them yes, I birthed them, but it was always my fault that my husband could not father children. For my wickedness with another man, the same man that fathered them. And now he hates me — he has turned on me all because I wanted the money."

"The money?" Truly, if Stefan wasn't so worried, he would have a half a mind to be confused. Was she merely mad or speaking truths?"

"Yes, we needed money. But we have money now, and we have a title. The curse is broken with you two married, but I could not allow you to be happy. I am sorry. I really am. But it would not be fair for you two to be happy while I have been sad and rejected all my life."

"Forgive me, but you've been given everything." Stefan argued. "A titled husband? Wealth? And children, regardless of where they came from."

"*Love!*" the witch yelled. "Acceptance! It's all I wanted from my husband, from Edward, or from his family. I received nothing. None of it. So I take from you what you took from me."

Stefan was dizzy with her speech. "And what did I take from you?"

"My husband. You killed him!"

Rosalind stirred. Stefan made a move to stand in front of her as she lay across the bed. No telling what her insane mother would do. Perhaps he was right, and she was the type to eat her own young.

"I did nothing of the sort." Stefan said in soothing tones. "He died of the curse, do you forget?"

"You rejected Rosalind! It killed him! His heart was weak! You killed him!" She manically waved the dagger in the air. "So I killed her. I have no care for those children; they may as well be adopted. Because of them, I was hated. You do not deserve to be happy. Now, we are even." With a laugh, she laid back down on the bed. "Yes, finally! Edward! I did it for you, Edward! We are even! And now we can be happy together…"

Rosalind stirred again. Stefan muffled a curse and looked out the window. How to escape without causing Rosalind harm or getting killed by the evil mother? A movement caught his eye.

Samson! Of course! He whistled and quickly thanked his lucky stars that his horse was in fact part human, or at least seemed to be as he lifted his head to unhook the branch his lead was tied to and walked slowly to the door.

Stefan made a promise to give Samson his body weight in

oats if they pulled this off.

Rosalind stirred again, and suddenly Stefan's memory brought forth pictures of their first meeting, when she fell into his arms. When the horrible curse started. If he could go back and change those words, he would. For it was never the idea of marriage that put him off, and now looking at her helpless body, he realized he would do anything and everything in his power to protect what was his. Even if it meant leaving.

Rosalind's mother shrieked and cackled as she kicked her feet on the bed. It was now or never. As quiet as possible, he lifted Rosalind into his arms, and noticing that he had mere seconds before the mom charged after him, he ran to the door threw it open and put Rosalind on Samson.

"Take her home boy, take her home." Rosalind's body was lying across Samson, she would be fine. The minute Samson trotted away; he heard a shriek as though from the pit of Hell emerge from the direction of the cottage.

He leapt out of the way just in time as the dagger flew from the witch's grasp, aimed straight for his heart.

Now, she was without a weapon. She ran at him eyes blazing. A shot rang in the distance, and the insane woman fell to the ground.

Mr. Fitzgerald dropped the pistol, his hands shaking. "I didn't know her madness had reached this far... I saw — I saw the horse and Rosalind..." He looked down at his hands then back at Stefan. "Did I kill her?"

With his heart beating wildly in his chest, Stefan checked the dowager's body for a pistol shot. "No, you hit her in the arm. She stirs even now. The walls of Bedlam will be the first thing she sees when she awakens."

CHAPTER TWENTY-TWO

The heart will break, but broken live on.
~ Lord Byron ~

ROSALIND'S MOUTH TASTED BITTER and dry. What had happened? The last thing she remembered was the wine and Stefan and…

"Stefan!" The blackness of the room brought terror rather than comfort. Where was he? Where was she?

Frantic, she looked around, not noticing anything familiar about her surroundings.

The door clicked open.

"How are you feeling?" Stefan's mother walked in with a worried expression plastered across her face.

"I…" Rosalind found she couldn't speak. "I'm not sure. Is Stefan here? Is he alright?"

The Dowager Duchess of Montmouth smiled. "Well. The last time I've seen him this worried was when his father died. Though he never took to spirits like he has now. I believe my son has also taken to talking to his horse." She smiled to herself and shook her head. "But I assure you, he will be fine. He survived a shipwreck after all. Now dear, how do you feel? Can you move?"

Rosalind tried to wiggle her toes. Everything felt right, except for the nagging tiredness that seemed to plague her body. "Was it another spell then?"

"The wine." The Dowager sat on the bed and patted Rosalind's hand. "Child, it seems your mother was trying to poison you and Stefan."

"But…" Rosalind's mind was barely able to wrap around the idea. "Surely she's mad, but to kill me? Her own daughter?"

"Bitterness does things that sometimes we do not understand, Rose. I've brought your godmother here to the house to attend to your needs. Your sister wasn't to be found anywhere on the estate, perhaps she was out."

Rosalind shifted, so Stefan hadn't told anyone of her sister's betrothal. "Isabelle is to be married to the new Earl of Harris. She left a day ago."

"I know, dear, and how sad that must be for you. But I was talking of Gwen, the sister with that raven black hair. She seems to be missing. It is of no matter though. I've told Stefan to locate her at once."

"Gone?" Gwen would never run away, would she? What if something happened to her? "And mother?"

"At Bedlam. Now rest dear. You both have done your jobs, the curse is broken, even Fitz is getting better."

Rosalind nodded and laid her head back on the pillow. She couldn't help but feel a nagging suspicion that things were far from over. With both sisters gone and the families' health returning, why did she feel so horrid? Granted, her own mother had tried to kill her, but she had been slowly going mad ever since her father died.

With a sigh, she fought to close her eyes. Perhaps Stefan

would have some answers upon his return.

CHAPTER TWENTY-THREE

There is no instinct like that of the heart.
~ Lord Byron ~

STEFAN CURSED AS HE kicked the desk in front of him. How had Gwen done it? The only clue they had of the whereabouts of the youngest sister was now with Gwen. And the middle sister was now traveling in search of her.

All of them under his protection. Both gone, and his wife had almost died. Could things possibly get worse? The only positive in the whole situation was that the curse seemed to have lifted. Fitz health was returning to normal, his mother was able to walk around without much help and Elaina was back to being Elaina.

Another problem he had no desire to look at. It seemed to be the woman's only joy in life to enrage Stefan with every word that dripped from her mouth. To think that he would even think of having an affair with the woman! He was married, as was she, and he didn't forget the haughty looks thrown between James and her when Fitz was on his death bed.

For the past hour he hadn't been able to bring himself to read the correspondence that had arrived in the post. The letters written in black sealed his fate as well as Rosalind's. He wondered, truly wondered, how it had come to this. The truth of Rosalind's birth was still pounding in his head. His conversation with the next in line to be married did nothing but make his mood plummet. After all this time, he had to believe there was some sort of hex on their family and if he didn't marry the rightful bloodline of the deceased earl, then everything would be for naught.

"Stefan?"

He turned to see James standing in the doorway, looking very much the dandy known to the ton.

"What is it?" He snapped.

"Mother says that the duchess has awoken. She asks for you." The butler handed James his hat and gloves.

Stefan's brow furrowed. "Where are you off to?"

James laughed. "Truly? You ask after all this madness has taken place? I have every intention of getting foxed and staying out all night in celebration. The curse is broken and I'm feeling better than I've felt in years. Perhaps I'll visit my mistresses, eh?"

Not the luckiest ladies in London, Stefan thought eyeing his dandified sod of a brother. "Yes, perhaps that would be best, after all. We wouldn't want Elaina getting too attached, hmm?"

"Nothing happened between us."

"So you say," Stefan muttered. "So you say."

James cursed. "What do you expect me to do? She threw herself at me! You wouldn't happen to be jealous, would you brother? After all, you've everything you need. A title, wealth, a wife... oh wait. Apologies, it seems your wife isn't technically in the best capacity to please you, is she? Well, I'm sure you can convince Elaina to attend to your baser needs."

Stefan pushed away from the desk and then charged his brother, ramming him into the nearest wall. "Speak poorly of my wife again and I'll put a bullet through you. Do you understand?"

James snorted, pushing Stefan off of him. "Oh I understand brother. Good day."

He sauntered off, leaving Stefan shaking from the whole episode. He needed to see Rosalind, but the last thing he wanted to do was admit that he had failed her. Yes, the curse was broken, but he wasn't even man enough to protect her sisters, nor would she be happy to find out that her father was not a blood relation but a stranger without a face.

With a sigh, he dragged his feet to the large stairway and slowly ascended. The woman had been put through so much, why was he always the cause of her pain?

Rosalind dreamt of the day she danced with Stefan in the snow. Of the playful way he teased her, and his horrid proposals and finally his kisses.

She awoke to the smell of hot biscuits and tea.

"That's it." Mary said sitting on the bed. "I knew a good cup of tea would wake you up, after all, it's said to have healing properties. Mr. Fitzgerald brought it over first thing this morning. Worried sick, he is."

Rosalind smiled, but didn't reach for the tea. But who could blame her? With nerves as strong as a feather she wanted nothing more than to see her husband and have a good cry. Well that, and perhaps a blood sizzling kiss.

"Ahem." A male voice came from the doorway.

"Stefan!" Rosalind didn't mean to yell, but she couldn't help the relief she felt at seeing his face.

"I see your voice hasn't met any harm, just as loud as ever. Ah Mary good to see you, do you per chance have our cane close by?"

Mary grunted and sauntered out of the room.

"I think she's beginning to like me," Stefan grinned and closed the door, locking it behind him. "How do you feel, Rose?"

Her breath hitched, which was all it took for Stefan to rush to her side and pull her into his arms. "I'm so sorry, Rose. I swear I'll make it better. I swear it."

"Just hold me."

"With pleasure." Stefan pushed the hair away from her eyes and kissed her eye lids. "I could not bear to lose you, Rose."

"Did she truly—"

"Your mother was mad, Rose. A sane woman would never cause her children harm."

Rosalind nodded.

"I need to tell you something, and I fear it isn't going to make you feel any better. Would you rather I waited until you were out of bed and walking?"

How much worse could it get? "Tell me now, please. Just promise not to let go of me."

"I believe I can manage." Stefan pulled her into his lap, cradling her head in the crook of his shoulder. "Your father..." He paused and looked away. "He was a good man."

Rosalind turned her head to look Stefan in the eye. "Yes." Her words were tentative. "Was that what you wanted to say?"

"For now..." Stefan bit his lip. "Well, that and both your sisters seem to be missing now. Gwen has gone after Isabelle. Apparently she understands more of that horrid language than she let on. For she took the betrothal contract with her. A note was left that she would return once she reached the location where Isabelle was taken. Unfortunately, she refused to tell us where that specific location was."

Rosalind shuddered. She should have known Gwen would do something like this. "We have to go after her."

"*We...* will do nothing. *I,* however, have plans to do exactly that." Stefan pushed the hair away from her brow and bent near to bestow a kiss upon her face. "There is something else."

Rosalind felt the all too familiar choking fear. "What is it?"

"I've failed you."

"How? I don't understand."

Stefan cursed. "Both your sisters are missing. I'm supposed to take care of you. How am I to do that when I cannot even take care of two young girls? Not to mention be outsmarted by them, but what's worse, what's worse..." he repeated and looked down. "Your father is not truly your father."

"I don't understand your meaning." A cold chill shook her core.

"The earl, who died — he was not your father. Your mother said as much when she tried to poison you."

"But how are you failing me?"

Stefan took a deep breath and released another string of curses. "As of today, your mother has broken her silence. I've tried to do my best Rosalind. But gossip is rampant that you and your sisters are bastards."

Rosalind gasped, and began to choke on her sobs. "But, my parents were married, they were..."

"Your parents, your true parents were not married Rosalind. Your father claimed you as his, but the damage my dear, has already been done."

"You cannot be married to me." Rosalind's voice shook. Her hands wrung the bed sheet as her mind tormented her with images of Stefan again and again.

"I'm not the true descendant, the one to break the curse am I?"

"For the last time, there is no curse, but you are correct. It apparently now falls to another woman, your cousin Maleficent."

Rosalind could not speak. Words would not come out of her mouth, not even when she tried to force her lips to move. "So the contract between our families…"

"The contract says I need to marry the true blood relation of the Earl of Hariss."

Rosalind pushed his hand away. "Then you must do as it says. You are, after all, a duke."

She kept her voice cold; she had to. How could she allow him to stay married to her? She wasn't even the way to solve the curse, if one existed, and now she had her doubts. Perhaps her mother was truly mad and poisoning everyone, herself included. It would make sense, which meant, Rosalind had no reason to truly be stayed to Stefan. Other than loving him with all her heart.

But he must never know.

Stubbornly, Rosalind pasted a smile on her face. "We will, of course, get our marriage annulled. No one will be the wiser that we spent the evening together, and if there is a child… Well, we will cross that bridge if it happens."

"Rose—" Stefan choked. "What are you saying?" Stefan began to pace around the room. "How can you say such things? I… I…" He cursed himself for not being able to say the words, but she was discarding him so quickly, so effectively. Had she no feelings for him at all? "I care for you deeply."

A tear ran down her cheek. "And I you. After all, you've been so good to me and my sisters."

"That's it? That's all you are going to say?" Stefan was incredulous and more pained than he ever thought possible.

Silence answered him. "Is this what you truly want, Rosalind? To be rid of me?"

"It is what is right."

Stefan cursed. "Devil take it! I don't give a wit for what is right, Rosalind. Do you not want to be married?"

His eyes betrayed him, the wound cut deep. But Rosalind couldn't find in herself to do anything except nod the affirmative. How could she saddle the great Duke of Montmouth to herself? How selfish could a person be? For it would only be for her own benefit; he would be shunned by society for not only marrying a bastard, but going against both their dying fathers' last wishes.

"Yes," she mouthed weakly.

Stifling an oath, he stormed off, slamming the door behind him.

CHAPTER TWENTY-FOUR

Where there is mystery, it is generally suspected there must also be
evil.
~ Lord Byron ~

ROSALIND'S LIPS QUIVERED AS the wet frigid air blasted against
her face. The temperature hadn't caused her quivering; no, it
was because she was hurting deeper than she ever thought
possible, and all because she was following her father's final
wish.

Stefan looked past her, closing his eyes as he said the
words that started everything. "I release you."

Rosalind found that she couldn't stop the sad smile from
spreading across her face. "Am I an animal then, Your Grace?
That begs to be released?" She closed her eyes against the
burning intrusion of tears.

"No," he choked. "You would never beg to be released
from anything, not my Rose. Not unless you asked, and I
know you better than you believe. You need no reminder of
the pain I have caused you, nor the nightmare of being with a

man who is more brute than gentleman."

"And if I want the brute?" she asked in a small voice.

"The brute wants you… will *always* want you."

Tears streamed down Rosalind's face, the salty invaders rolled down her lips. "I lo—"

"It's time my lady," Mr. Fitzgerald said. "Up you go! We'll get you back to the country estate, make it right as rain, we will."

"Be happy, Rose."

Words would not come… tears, however, streamed of their own accord as the vision of her husband disappeared down the road. He said he would protect her at all costs. She hadn't realized the cost would be that of her heart.

Within a few hours, Stefan was so drunk he wasn't able to see straight. The whiskey wasn't doing its job, at least he didn't feel it was, for he could still remember the sad smile spread across Rosalind's face. He wanted her. He loved her. But, if she truly loved him, would she not have asked him to fight for her? To stay with her forever and always? Was he merely talking romantic nonsensical things because his heart was so heavily involved?

In an effort to make his mood worse, he stumbled to the room where Rosalind had been staying and laid across the bed, taking in her scent. The tea cup was still full. The girl hadn't touched it.

Obsessively, he held it to his lips thinking that if she had touched it, he wanted to feel her lips against his, imagine it once again.

A strong odor greeted him, so foul his stomach churned. What the devil had they put in her tea? Suspicion pooled in his belly. On a whim, most likely because he was foxed and depressed, he called for the maid.

"Yes?" She gave a low curtsy never lifting her eyes to his face.

"Who brought the tea?"

"Mr. Fitzgerald, sir, he says it has healing properties."

"It's foul," he remarked absentmindedly.

She let out a giggle. "Yes, I think the rats agree with you, for some of this concoction took a spill earlier tonight, and they died instantly, most likely from that awful smell."

"What did you say?"

"The putrid smell, sir?" she answered.

"Before that?"

"The rats?"

"Yes." He rose from the bed and walked to her. "They died? All of them?"

"Well, yes, but they could have gotten into some poison too, sir…"

Stefan's memory flashed ahead of him. The tea, always the tea. Hadn't he suspected as much before? Mr. Fitzgerald was bringing his family tea, when they were ill. Even Rosalind's mother, and the night of Rosalind's spell.

"Oh, God…" Stefan prayed as he stumbled out of the room and called for his horse. "Oh, God, oh, God, please let her be alive."

CHAPTER TWENTY-FIVE

"O true apothecary!
Thy drugs are quick. Thus with a kiss, I die."
~ Romeo, Romeo and Juliet ~

ROSALIND WISHED FOR ONE of her spells to come upon her again, for no other reason than to sleep away the pain stabbing at her chest.

To be forever separated from the man she loved, could anything be worse?

The carriage pulled to a stop. Mary reached across and patted her hand. "T'will be alright, you'll see. My Alfred won't let the duke be so hair-brained for long, you'll see."

"Your Alfred?" Rosalind was partially amused. "Is that where you were running off to so often?"

A blush rose to Mary's cheeks. "It isn't proper to talk of such things. Your duke will come for you. I know it in my bones."

"He isn't my duke." Rosalind sighed. "Not anymore."

"My lady?" Willard held out his hand. With reluctance,

she grasped it as he helped her out of the carriage.

Her country estate mocked her with its dark and gothic scenery. The last thing she wanted to do was walk into an empty home. It reminded her of her heart, her soul. Black and empty for Stefan had taken every ounce of love she had, and she feared she had nothing left to give, to anyone.

Her sisters were still missing, though Stefan promised that they would surely be found. He had sent men in both directions after them.

So now, Rosalind was left to live out the rest of her days in a dark castle with no one save her godmother and her family's odd valet.

It was still strange that he decided to escort them back to the estate. After all, he was now in charge of the London home, but he had been so worried. She was at least grateful that the man cared.

The air within the house was frigid, void of any warmth. With a sigh, she notified Mr. Fitzgerald and Mary that they would all share the task of lighting the fires. She helped Mary with the downstairs while Mr. Fitzgerald brought in everyone's trunks.

Exhausted, Rosalind sauntered up to her room, but stopped when she noted none of the bedrooms had any fires going. With a sigh, she walked into Mr. Fitzgerald's bedroom and began the tedious task.

She jerked at the old fireplace and lost her balance sending her sailing into the desk near her. A flutter of papers flew to the floor. Swearing, Rosalind bent to retrieve them and froze.

Edward Willard Fitzgerald, the correspondence said.

A chill ran down her spine. Perhaps it was merely a coincidence, perhaps...

"My lady..."

Mr. Fitzgerald's smile froze on his face, then disappeared

altogether. Fortunately, Rosalind was back at the fireplace even though the papers were still scattered.

"Yes, Willard? Sorry, I closed the window because a breeze came through. I was just going to right the papers once I finished with the fire." She did her best to sound cheerful though her hands were shaking something terrible.

"No," he said curtly. "That will not be necessary. Why don't you go take a rest, dear?"

"If you think that's what is best..." Rosalind brushed past him, hiding the note in her skirts as she did so.

By the time she reached her room, her heart was fluttering like a butterfly. She had to warn Mary, they had to get out of there, they needed...

A knock on the door jolted her. With a startled scream, she scolded herself then opened the door.

Mr. Fitzgerald was on the other side, tea in hand.

"Oh good, I'm so very glad you took my advice. Would you care for some tea to warm your bones? Perhaps it may even help you sleep a deep sleep, Rosalind."

"Of course," Rosalind smiled kindly and reached for the tea, willing her hand to stop shaking as she thanked him again and shut the door.

The tea smelt heavenly. It was too good to resist. She took a sip, and then another. After two or three sips her body began to feel heavy. Sleep, it seemed was finally going to overtake her, and make her pain go away. With a smile she stumbled to her bed, but didn't make it, as she crashed to the floor and blackness overtook her.

CHAPTER TWENTY-SIX

"When beggars die there are no comets seen;
The heavens themselves blaze forth the death of princes."
~ *Julius Caesar* — *William Shakespeare* ~

"SAMSON! TRULY BOY, YOU need to go faster!" Stefan had been riding through the night. Samson, good horse that he was hadn't complained, only went faster and faster. He had no desire to run his own horse to the ground, but found that he had no other option. So he prayed his horse would not die on the excursion.

Rosalind would always come before Samson, so he explained quite plainly what the trip would mean to the horse. But if anything, the horse seemed to puff its chest out wider than before and nodded in understanding.

"Good man." Stefan patted Samson again. His horse neighed and picked up speed.

They reached the estate by morning. Samson appeared exhausted. The minute Stefan hopped off, he sent Samson to the stables. The horse slowly trotted off in the general direction.

Stefan took the stairs two at a time and burst through the doors.

"Rosalind!" he yelled, his voice echoed off the walls. Where was everybody? Mary? Cook? And the evil Mr. Fitzgerald.

"Rosalind!" He tried again in vain. It was morning; surely they were breaking their fast. He rushed into the kitchen. The kettle was boiling over and cook appeared to be sleeping across the table. He shook her awake, but she merely opened one eye and closed it again without answering him.

"Blast!" He ran out of the kitchens and up to the bedrooms.

Bursting into Rosalind's room, he stopped dead when his eyes took in the scene. Rosalind lay across the floor, appearing to be sleeping peacefully. And Mr. Fitzgerald cleaned a dagger by the window.

"Ah, so the prince comes to rescue the princess, does he?" Mr. Fitzgerald let out a bark of laughter.

"You!" Stefan roared. "It was you the whole time! There was no curse!"

"Only the curse that Rosalind's mother brought into the family. I so wanted my love to be happy. So I gave her everything she wanted, even when she married the late earl. So very tragic, his accident. The man didn't even taste the hemlock as it claimed his sorry excuse for a life."

"Why kill him?"

"Because she started to care for him, why else?" Mr. Fitzgerald smiled and closed his eyes. "You see, I've been slowly poisoning the family for years. I wanted the earl to be unable to father children. He did, however, father two. Rosalind and Gwendolyn. Isabelle was a creature of my own making, though she never knew. Her mother, bless her soul, was so easily manipulated. I poisoned her against her husband, told her he was not able to father children. The family of course blamed her, so I offered her an escape. We could continue our love in secret. I would be the rightful father and when the time was right, we would threaten to expose the secret and run away together."

Stefan made a move towards Rosalind, but Mr. Fitzgerald pointed the dagger at Stefan. "Confession is good for the soul, don't you agree?"

"Of course."

"I mean to confess my sins before I kill you. It would be polite after keeping you in suspense for so long."

"Then by all means," Stefan ground out, waiting until the perfect time before he strangled the man and sent him to his eternal punishment.

"She fell in love with him. It was slow — she tried to hide it from me. So I killed him. She was unable to get over the death, so I began to give her tea. I began to poison her mind with lies. Truly, it was so easy to confuse the woman it hardly seemed fair, so lost was she in her pain. I even convinced her that she helped kill her husband. It was too easy to allow her to nearly kill Rosalind. You see, if the mother was crazy, the fingers would not be pointed in my direction."

"And now?" Stefan asked.

"Now," Mr. Fitzgerald laughed. "Now I'm rich. All of my daughters are gone or will be the minute I drive my dagger into Rosalind's heart. For I hate her the most of them all. She looks like her father the most, and she held his heart in her hand. She had his love. I never got to experience love from my daughters because the countess refused to tell anyone."

"Jealousy is a sad excuse for murder."

"Murder," Mr. Fitzgerald said, "is never an excuse. It's an ending. A finale. And it's the only way to keep everyone silent. Unfortunately, Rosalind's sleeping spells were happening less often, she became too accustomed to the tea. I imagine only her body sleeps now when she is exposed to it. In her sleep, she hears all. But she is paralyzed. Do you know how frightening it must be for a woman to hear about her death, yet be unable to do a thing about it? Though I don't claim to be a botanist, I've read that the body can almost become frozen in this state."

Mr. Fitzgerald pulled out a pistol and aimed it at Stefan as he slowly walked to Rosalind's side.

"I killed your father, my sweet. I sold your sister, and provoked the other to run away. I destroyed everything, and now I will kill the man you love."

Stefan ducked just before the pistol went off.

Mr. Fitzgerald swore as Stefan's body rammed into his. The dagger came slashing about Stefan's face. With love driving him, Stefan grasped the blade of the dagger, letting it dig into his skin as blood trickled down his wrist, and slowly twisted it towards Mr. Fitzgerald's throat.

Shaking, he slowly pushed it in until no life was left in the man's cold eyes. With an oath he pushed away and ripped some of his clothing to cover the deep cuts.

"Rose," he whispered as he sat across the bed. "Rose, come back to me. Awake, my sleeping beauty."

His lips brushed across hers as a single tear slid down her cheek.

"I love you," he choked. "I love you so much."

Blue eyes flashed at him, and the beauty mouthed. "I love you, too."

CHAPTER TWENTY-SEVEN

She's beautiful, and therefore to be wooed;
She is woman, and therefore to be won.
~ Henry VI, Part I — Shakespeare ~

ROSALIND HAD NEVER BEEN so terrified, as when she overheard all the horrendous actions Mr. Fitzgerald had taken against her family and his own flesh and blood. She still shivered when she thought upon it.

Rest was the last thing she wanted, especially now that she knew she wasn't dying and that her sleeping spells had been caused by nightshade in her tea. A botanist, Mr. Fitzgerald, or Edward was not, for he hadn't realized a person could become used to the stuff in small doses. His greatest mistake was in trying to trick Rosalind into thinking she was dying, when really the plant was only dangerous in large doses and only if injected.

A chill ran down her spine when she thought of the other plants found in his possession. Monkshood being one of them. She would have surely died had he given her something more potent, and she was suddenly thankful that he had been thinking he was harming her with nightshade instead of the more poisonous plant.

The orangery smelled delightful, she let herself in and closed her eyes. A male voice began to hum. Surely that wasn't Stefan, that would be too romantic, it would be—

"—Have I found you? The one who makes me sing? Once upon a midnight dream…" Rosalind followed the voice as it became louder. "As I lay me down to sleep, my midnight dream I know will keep. The stars in your eyes tell me what your heart is afraid to say. That while I wait for my prince, he will one day say…"

She turned the corner and smiled. Stefan was down on one knee, roses in hand. He stopped singing and cleared his throat.

"My love…"

"Oh, good start," Rosalind commented, laughing.

"Yes, I thought so, too." Stefan smiled. "My love." He winked. "With lips as red as a rose, eyes as blue as the sea, I find I cannot keep myself from wanting thee."

"And it rhymes! How very poetic," Rosalind couldn't help saying.

"Yes well, I've worked on it all day. Now, may I continue?"

She nodded.

"Where was I? Oh yes, I find I cannot keep myself from wanting thee. When I close my eyes, all my mind conjures up is pictures of you. My perfect Rose. My love, you are my little dove."

"Little dove?"

Stefan squirmed. "Yes, well, it rhymed with love."

Rosalind's heart burst with joy. How she loved this man! "Pray, continue."

"Yes." He cleared his throat again and looked at the paper, then cursed and threw it to the ground. In two steps he was in front of her, pulling her roughly against his chest as his mouth slanted possessively across hers. "I cannot exist without you."

He kissed her until she felt her knees would buckle, his tongue teased hers in a game of domination and devotion. "I cannot breathe without you."

His hands reached savagely into her hair, pulling it out of its pins as he moaned against her lips. "I am lost without you."

"Stefan," she gasped as his hands dipped into her bodice.

"Yes?" He sounded distracted as he pulled away her dress and corset.

"It seems you've discovered how to woo."

With a laugh, he stripped her upper torso of any clothing. "All I needed was some inspiration."

Rosalind let out a laugh as his lips claimed her throat.

"We must marry at once," he joked.

With a burst of laughter, Rosalind pulled at his jacket. "Well, since you asked so nicely..."

"Come here." He plundered her mouth as his hands roamed across her silky skin. "I love you, I love you, I love you."

"And I love you," Rosalind choked out as a tear ran down her face.

"No more talking," Stefan ordered as he dragged her to the nearest table and pushed the plants onto the floor, making the pots shatter. With little effort the lifted her onto the table and used slow languid movements to show her exactly what he'd rather be doing.

EPILOGUE

"YOUR GRACE?" ALFRED CLEARED his throat several times before continuing. It was strange to see him out by the stables; he looked so horribly out of place. Stefan had half a mind to feel sorry for him. Was the man shaking? Unfortunately the near death experiences as well as the murders taking place under Rosalind's roof did nothing but make Stefan paranoid about anything and everything.

"Yes, is something wrong, Alfred? You look ill?"

"Ahem." Alfred gave Samson a nervous pat. "I am in need help, Your Grace."

"What is it?" Stefan leaned in close. "A debt? Have you been gambling? Trouble with the law? Truly, I would do anything for you, Alfred. You need but ask."

"I'm in love."

"Yes, well, anything but that. Now, try. What can I help you with?" Stefan was the last person in London from whom his valet should be seeking advice. Had the man missed the past month when Stefan's proposals set Rosalind to laughter and angered her enough to want to throttle him?

Just then Rosalind happened upon the two of them.

Alfred stared at the ground.

Stefan pulled at his cravat.

"What's going on?" she asked sweetly, though Stefan knew the look in her eyes was anything but sweet. Mocking? Yes. Sweet? Absolutely not.

"Talking of weather, and horses—"

"I'm in love!" Alfred blurted, even though Stefan was shaking his head in protest.

Rosalind sent Stefan a glare before reaching out and patting Alfred's hand. "Now, does the lovely lady know where your affections lie?"

"Oh, I'm sure if it! I just do not know how to go about this whole proposal business."

Rosalind burst out laughing. "And you thought to ask him?" She pointed a shaky hand at Stefan and leaned against Samson all the while wiping tears from her eyes. It wasn't long before Alfred too joined in the merriment. That left Stefan without an ally, for Samson was caught between the two with that gleaming smile on his face that was always mocking his master.

"Alright, that's enough," Stefan said sourly. "I can very well propose. I was nervous! That's all."

"Aw, it does these ears proud to hear so much laughter coming from the stables. What seems to be so funny?" Mary entered the stables hands on hips.

"Oh, my husband, he seems to be giving advice on how to woo." Rosalind winked and pulled Stefan close to her. He went because he couldn't very well deny his beautiful wife anything, even when she was laughing at his expense.

Suddenly, Alfred seemed to tense. He began to wring his hands in front of him like a nervous school boy. A grin spread across Stefan's face; he had quite an idea as to whom his valet held affection for.

"Alfred? Do you have anything you wish to say?" Stefan asked.

Alfred was pale and fidgety Devil take it, he couldn't back down now! It was the perfect set up. He gave Alfred a curt nod of encouragement. The valet swallowed and turned to Mary taking her hand within his.

"We shall marry at once."

"Oh, Good Lord above," Rosalind said next to him. "Have you been taking lessons from my husband? Alfred, that is not how one proposes. That is—"

"Oh yes, yes, yes!" Mary squealed with delight and kissed Alfred soundly on the mouth, much to Stefan's horrified dismay.

He cleared his throat.

The kiss continued.

"For the love of—"

"Sorry, Your Grace." Alfred pulled away, his cheeks slightly pink.

Rosalind snorted behind him, giving the clear message that he of all people shouldn't be the one to talk, after he so blatantly kissed her at last night's ball. Much to Lord Rawlings' and the Duke of Tempest's amusement, for they also had the occasional difficulty trying to keep their hands off their wives in public.

"If Your Graces will excuse us?" Alfred asked tactfully.

"You are dismissed," Stefan said firmly. The two bounded away from the stables hand in hand.

Rosalind reached around him hugging his body from behind. He smiled and turned around to kiss her firmly on the mouth, then led his wife away from the dirty stables to the comfort of his study. Once they reached his destination he pulled Rosalind into his arms. Pure contentment caused his muscles to relax as he breathed in her scent.

"Any word of my sisters?" she asked once they had

enjoyed the silence of each other's presence for a while..

Stefan sighed, leaning into his wife's embrace. "Not just yet, but they are safe, I know it in my heart."

Rosalind sighed and pulled away. She walked to the door and Stefan had to fight his irritation that she would leave him while he so desperately wanted to have her on his very desk.

She turned the lock.

"Thank the saints." He swept her into his arms pushing her back against the door, savagely stripping her of her afternoon dress.

"Ah, *tsk-tsk*! Remember, you said you would woo me even after we were married, you brute. Now, give me the words, give me the sonnets, and give me the flowers."

Stefan whispered naughty words into his wife's ear.

With a giggle, she answered, "That will do nicely for now."

ABOUT THE AUTHOR

Rachel Van Dyken is the *New York Times*, *Wall Street Journal*, and *USA Today* bestselling author of over 29 books. She is obsessed with all things Starbucks and makes her home in Idaho with her husband and two snoring boxers.

OTHER BOOKS BY RACHEL VAN DYKEN

The Bet Series
The Bet (Forever Romance)
The Wager (Forever Romance)
The Dare

Eagle Elite
Elite (Forever Romance)
Elect (Forever Romance)
Entice
Elicit

Seaside Series
Tear
Pull
Shatter
Forever
Fall
Strung

Wallflower Trilogy
Waltzing with the Wallflower
Beguiling Bridget
Taming Wilde

London Fairy Tales
Upon a Midnight Dream
Whispered Music
Upon a Midnight Dream
When Ash Falls

Renwick House
The Ugly Duckling Debutante

The Seduction of Sebastian St. James
The Redemption of Lord Rawlings
An Unlikely Alliance
The Devil Duke Takes a Bride

Ruin Series
Ruin
Toxic
Fearless
Shame (October 6, 2014)

Other Titles
The Parting Gift
Compromising Kessen
Savage Winter
Divine Uprising
Every Girl Does It

Coming Soon
Capture (Seaside Pictures 1)
Eternal (The Seaside Series)
The Consequence of Loving Colton
The Consequence of Revenge
Ember
Feral Spring
Alexander King
The Challenge
Rip